CARVER COUNTY LIBRARY

THE PRIDE OF TEXAS

Also by

DUSTY RICHARDS

THE PRIDE OF TEXAS

DUSTY RICHARDS

GALWAY

OGHMA CREATIVE MEDIA

www.oghmacreative.com

ISBN: 978-1-63373-319-0

Interior Design by Casey W. Cowan
Editing by Gil Miller & Regina Hankins

Galway Press
Oghma Creative Media
Bentonville, Arkansas
www.oghmacreative.com

For Jodi Thomas

ACKNOWLEDGEMENTS

MANY THANKS CONTINUE to go to my publisher, Oghma Creative Media. This outfit just continues to exceed my expectations, and they're building a real solid body of work. They seem to have a talent for turning stories nobody wanted into award-winning books. They did it with *The Mustanger and the Lady*, and they may well do it again with this one. An old cowboy can only hope.

In particular, I want to give a big thanks to the head honcho and design guru over there, Casey Cowan, and his right-hand woman, Venessa Cerasale. I'd also like to thank the editing crew—Gil Miller, Regina Hankins, Gordon Bonnet, George "Clay" Mitchell, and Michael Frizell. Thanks also to Amy Howk, who keeps the whole thing riding on the rails, and my buddy Velda Brotherton, who convinced me to take a chance with these *hombres* when they were just getting started.

Thanks for taking the time to read with me. Feel free to drop me a line anytime at dustyrichards@cox.net. I love hearing from my fans, and I'll always reply.

—*Dusty Richards*
Springdale, Arkansas
August 1, 2017

ACKNOWLEDGEMENTS

ONE

HEAT WAVES WARPED the bloody sunset on the west Texas horizon. Seated on the dusty ground beside his twin brother Jackson, Andrew Franks hugged the knees of his patched overalls, the knot in the center of his stomach growing larger and harder. In the distance, his pa ranted and raged at their mother in the nearby house. They were arguing again. His pa never took anyone or anything that stood up to him in a good way, least of all from Nancy, his wife—or either of their sixteen-year-old twins.

"We ought to—" Jackson stopped abruptly.

"We've tried that before," Andrew said under his breath. And they got their asses busted. And she got beat as well for defending them. No, they needed to wait till Pa was over his fit. That meant they'd have to sleep all night out in the brush—by morning Pa might be cooled down. That couldn't come quick enough—the old man simmering down.

Pa'd been on a tear for two days. It all started when his good gray horse Colonel colicked and died. It was one of those things that happened. The gelding got too hot working cattle. Pa rode him in hard to the ranch and Colonel drank too much water, laid down an hour later, and twisted a gut—then he died. Horses do those sorts of things. Pa'd blamed the two of them for letting his prize gelding die. The next day, while the three of them were gone from the ranch house catching maverick cattle, a sow rooted over his sour mash barrel that was up on a stand and he blamed their mother for letting that happen. Two dollars' worth of corn and sugar spilled out on the ground. Pa never held with any waste.

The red sow had probably used one of the mesquite-post legs of the barrel-stand to rub her itchy back on and that was how she upset it. Anyway when the three of them rode in that evening, they discovered her and three shoats wallowing in the stinking mess. They were as full of his sour mash as ticks. Andrew recalled closing his eyes in surrender at the sight of the sow sitting up on her hind legs and grunting at the old man.

She should never have done that. Andrew watched Pa take out his Navy model .44 and began busting caps at her. The wounded sow ran away screaming her lungs out. Pa's green-broke horse threw him off. He landed on his butt in the puddle of sour mash. He shouted for the boys to go get her and cut her throat.

"We'll butcher her tonight."

Grateful to escape his wrath, Andrew nodded to his brother and they pounded their bare heels in the sides of their ponies and set off into the cedar and live oak to find the wounded sow.

Fifty yards from the homestead, Jackson gave him a big grin and laughed. "I'm glad we didn't stay there a minute longer. I was cracking up. Him on his butt in that stinking crud—"

"Shut up. He may hear you. We better find that sow, or it'll be our hides next." Expecting to see the old man right behind them, Andrew looked back in dread but when he checked, there was no sign of him. By this time, their mother must be catching all kinds of hell.

"That sow went this way." Jackson waved him to the right and up a dry wash. "She's got more holes in her than a sieve. She can't be far."

In minutes, they found the pig lying on her side in a shallow wash, gasping her last. Andrew tossed the reins to his brother and swung down. He took the skinning knife out of the sheath on his hip, walked over, and stabbed it to the hilt into her throat. Despite his jump back after the thrust, the bloody flow from her jugular splashed over his pants legs and bare feet. With a frown of disgust at the mess, he wiped the blade on his britches and put it back in the sheath.

Jackson came over with the horses and offered him the end of his riata. "We can slide her along on the ground, can't we?"

"Sure." Andrew nodded and ignored her hind legs kicking in the last throes of her life to loop the braided rawhide rope around them. He gave a nod for Jackson to take up slack with his pony. Satisfied the hitch would work, he ran to his own horse, took the reins, and nodded toward the house as he swung up.

There was lots of water to boil. They'd have to build a big fire under the large scalding kettle. It would be hours before that water would ever be hot enough. Then they'd have to shave and gut her, then cut up the carcass and salt down the meat to save it. All before bedtime. Pa hated waste.

The sounds of Pa's swearing and ongoing rage grew louder as they came closer to the house. They hunkered down by the corral, hoping to miss his wrath. It was all Andrew could do not to put his hands over his ears to cut the sound of her screaming—hearing her cry out as Pa struck her again and again. From the corner of his eye, Andrew saw Jackson was fixing to get up and do something. His hand shot out and he restrained his brother.

"Ain't nothing we can do."

His words were sharper than he even intended.

"By gar, there's got to be something. I can't take much more of him hurting her like that."

"You'll only make it worse on her and us."

Jackson nodded, face grim, and settled back on his butt in defeat, resting his chin on his arms supported by his knees. "We won't be kids forever. We won't have to live under him forever. You and me, we could cut out now."

"He'd blame her for that, too."

"Yeah, we'd have to take her along too, wouldn't we?"

Andrew nodded. No way they could leave her behind to his rabid wrath. Any more, he'd found that he could personally shed Pa's beatings. The old man knew that, too, and the fact only made him angrier.

"Reckon the water's hot enough by now in that big kettle to shave her?" Jackson asked about the pending sow's slaughter.

"Be after dark before it gets that hot."

"I may eat her liver raw like them Injuns do the buffalo."

"I couldn't eat it or anything even if I had to."

Jackson rubbed his belly under the tattered shirt. "Hurts me too—damn him. You hearing her screams?"

Andrew nodded.

Then two shots rang out. Both boys sprang to their feet and looked across the corral in the direction of the post-walled house. They searched each other's faces.

"What did he do now?"

Andrew shook his head. No telling. The nausea rose behind his tongue and he tried to swallow it. His eyes grew pained with sorrow. Filled with indecision, his ears were struck by another shot and a crashing of dishes.

"What in hell's he doing with that damn gun?" Jackson asked from beside him as they ran for the house.

"It ain't good. It won't be good," Andrew said over and over as they both raced for the canvas-roofed shack.

Stopped at the open doorway veiled in blue gun smoke, they searched each other for who'd be first. Without a word, Andrew led the way inside. The sight of the lifeless bearded face of Pryor

Franks lying on the floor, with the dark bullet hole in his forehead seeping blood, caused Andrew to block his brother's way.

"He's dead."

"Oh, dear Jesus—where's Ma?" His brother was trying to see past him.

"Sit down, Jackson." Andrew turned out a chair for him.

"He kilt her, didn't he? Didn't he?"

Andrew forced him down. The effort sent a torrent of tears from his brother's face as he accepted the seat. Jackson's fists jammed to eyes, he began mumbling how he should have come to help her.

"Get hold of yourself." Andrew stepped around the table in the dark house to discover her still body. When he knelt beside her crumpled form to feel for a pulse, he found dark blood covering the top of her dress. God bless her, he figured she'd probably forgiven him for shooting her before she died.

Jackson stomped his bare feet on the hard-packed dirt floor. "We should have come. Andrew! We should have come."

Andrew took a deep breath through his nose, trying to ignore the sulfur stink of gunsmoke and the coppery odor of blood and death. Then he shook his head. "No, Jackson, he'd of just killed us too."

TWO

JUDGE EARL WATKINS had a rusty voice that ranged from high pitched to a deep low bass. When he flailed his lazy, white burro on the butt with the stick and shouted at him, his voice sounded like he was in a deep well. But when he went to talking to the two of them, it came out high-pitched.

"Why would your father ever do a thing like this?"

"He was mad about the sow." Andrew trotted his horse along beside the burro as it shot ahead, then went slow until the white-whiskered man under the top hat beat him again with his stick, then he flew ahead of their horses. It was a see-saw ride accompanying the justice of the peace back to their ranch under the stars.

Judge Watkins was the law in those parts and Andrew figured the authorities better see their mess. No need in folks thinking they'd killed the old man. He wanted it all on the up and up. This strange, whiny-voiced old man in his rumpled black suit, string tie around his open collar, and his pot belly riding on the big wooden horn of his ole Mexican saddle would do what was necessary. Andrew was tired of his brother, who kept making faces of disagreement behind Watkins's back.

After they'd butchered and salted down the hog meat and laid the two corpses out on boards, they spent the rest of the night riding over to the Los Olivos Saloon and Store to find Watkins.

In the predawn, when they first arrived at the Store and Saloon, they found Watkins asleep under a quilt in a rocking chair on the porch. Andrew's horse snorted from behind the hitch rack in front of Watkins. That must have startled him, for he swept the quilt back and shoved a sawed-off shotgun in their faces.

"What in the hell do you boys want this time of night?" He looked hard at them, then uncocked the right hammer and set it on the porch floor. "Sorry, boys, but you never know who's going to sneak up on you 'round here."

"Yes, sir, judge. We come to get you. Our pa—well, he got too mad last night and he shot maw and then hisself."

"Aw, boys that's a terrible thing." Watkins looked at them out of pain-filled eyes and shook his head real slow, then reset that top hat again—a little to the left side of center. "I guess I better go up and hold a coroner's jury."

"Yes sir. We wanted you to see them—we wasn't sure—I mean what we were supposed to do."

"Boys, boys, you two done the right thing. I need to go look it over. Now one of you go saddle my old burro, Jasper T. Simmons, over there in the pen and I'll go tell her where I'm going."

Jackson swung his horse out. "I can get your burro."

"Mind you he kicks." Watkins waved a finger at him.

"I know all about burros," Jackson assured him and rode his pony across the dusty ground to the stick and post corral.

Andrew stepped off the saddle and hitched his mount to the rack. With a stiff back from butchering, he reached for the starry sky and yawned. Been a long night for him working up the sow, plus the ride over there and it wasn't through yet. The burial they faced later on that day was the thing he dreaded the worst. No telling how Jackson would take it all. His brother would never get over the fact the two of them didn't try to stop the old man. Andrew climbed on the porch and looked back—Jackson had the burro caught—fine. He went on through the dark doorway and into the sour aroma of liquor and cigar smoke.

A dark brown bar went down the left side. Some old mirrors were on the back bar and a few paintings of near-naked women were pasted up on them. Hard to see the nudes in the dim light and the judge was coming back talking ninety to nothing in Spanish to the short, swarthy-faced woman beside him.

"This is one of Pryor Franks's boys."

She nodded and crossed herself. "I am so sorry such a bad thing happened to you."

Watkins said, "There's two of them. They look alike."

She nodded and swallowed hard. "My English, she isn't no good. Tell your brother what I say no?"

"I will, ma'am." Andrew had his hat off for her. She was lots younger than her husband.

"Good. What will you do now?" She busied herself straightening up the judge's suit and fussing over him like he was going to make an appearance.

"Run the ranch I guess. We ain't got anything else."

Watkins cleared his throat to take over the conversation. "We'll need to find some relative to help you two. You'll need an adult to do your business. You boys are minors."

"I can't imagine who that would be." Andrew turned up his hands. All the kin he knew about they'd left behind in Arkansas even before the war broke out. Pa got real upset about folks telling him he had to pick a side—he got so mad he come home one night, loaded up their belongings in two wagons, and they came to Texas.

"Aw, you'll think of someone." Watkins ran his thumbs up and down under his suspenders. "We'll have to find you a guardian somewheres."

"Yes, sir." Andrew turned and told her thank you in Spanish, then slapped on his floppy hat. The judge acted like he was anxious to get going to the ranch.

"Your burro's saddled," Jackson said from the open doorway.

"We're coming, sonny. We're coming right now."

She asked the judge in Spanish when he'd be coming home. Watkins turned and told her he didn't know and shook his head hard enough he had to reset his top hat.

Outside, he led the burro up alongside the porch and then jumped on the saddle. The burro made a wild dash for the pen, but the judge finally turned him around with the reins and profanity. His low-cut shoes in the stirrups, he nodded for them to take the lead and began beating "what's his name" on the butt with a short stiff stick in the catch-up-and-stop gait.

They watered their horses about ten o'clock at a spring with a rock tank—they and their dad had built that structure. Watkins admired the work, drinking water from a tin cup he kept tied on his saddle. Andrew noticed his cup idea and decided he'd have to have one of them. They'd do to drink from or cook *pinole* in it.

Watkins got a handful of dry crackers out of his suit coat pocket and offered part of them to the boys. They took some and thanked him.

"I been thinking about what you boys'll do while I'm looking for you some relative."

"Looking for a relative?" Jackson made a face at the judge's back and Andrew frowned him down. They didn't need to upset the man.

"We can cook *and* sew. Why, last night we salted down a whole hog Pa shot yesterday," Andrew assured him. "We've got provisions and plenty of work to do."

"But—well, you're just boys." Judge gripped his chin under the whiskers and shook his head in wonderment.

Andrew frowned his brother down again. "We've been doing a man's work since we were ten. We can run that ranch and we aim to."

"You will still need an adult to do your business. That's Texas law, pure and simple."

Red-faced, Jackson started for the man. "To hell with Texas law, then!"

Andrew stopped him. "He's only doing what the law says he has to do."

"He's right, son. All I'm only doing is what the statutory laws of Texas says I must do."

The younger boy turned on his heel, fuming mad, and walked over to check on his girth.

"Jackson never meant nothing by that. It's been a helluva night for both of us."

Judge nodded his head and led his burro up by the tank to fork him. "Jasper T., you sorry rascal. Get up here. Now whoa. Now whoa, Jasper T. Simmons! Hold still!"

Jackson was already mounted and rode on ahead by himself. Andrew wished he'd had a chance to talk some sense into his brother on how to act, at least until Watkins left. After they got through Watkins's trial—or the "hearing," as he called it—and buried their parents, why, that old man would ride back home and forget who they were. Watkins had lots more important things to take care of. Like that Mexican woman and his bar with the naked women's pictures pasted on the mirrors. Lots more to fret over than two sixteen-year-olds and a two-bit, dried up cactus ranch. If Jackson didn't ruin it, they'd have a good chance to stay on their own place and go on like nothing had ever happened. Somehow he *had* to get his brother in line.

And quickly, too.

THREE

THE JUDGE WALKED back and forth across the hot, breathless room. "You boys never heard what he said to her?"

"He was yelling and shouting and cussing. It sounded like he always did when he was mad. But we never figured it would end like this." The smell of death was worse than ever in Andrew's nostrils.

Watkins made a pained look at Andrew. "And he was that mad about the sow turning over his sour mash barrel?"

"Aw, hell," Jackson said in disgust, seated outside the front door and hugging his knees. "He whipped the fire out of Andrew and me both one time for using a new nail on the roof when there were plenty of bent ones left to straighten."

"Hmmm." Watkins scratched his chin and snuffed out his nose. "He must have been mentally deranged."

"You could say that again." Then Jackson went into his mimicking the old man. "'Waste not, want not.' If I ever hear that quoted to me again I think I'll puke."

"You boys have a grave dug?"

"No." Andrew hoped the hearing was nearly over.

"You better start one." The judge hurried outside to

take a deep breath of air. He mopped his sweaty face with a handkerchief. "Murder and a suicide."

"Get the shovel," Andrew said to his brother, who struggled up and headed for the barn.

They had the grave dug by sundown. A common one, but it was six feet deep. Andrew wasn't having any varmints dig them up or Injuns either. He and Jackson were both exhausted when they climbed up the ladder and nodded to the judge seated on the chair that it was complete. Watkins had spent the day on his butt, mopping his sweaty face and giving them advice.

"I'll read some psalms," the judge said.

Jackson and Andrew went for the bodies wrapped in flannel sheets. First Pa's, then Ma's. They lowered them down under the judge's directions to be careful with the dead. Andrew wasn't sure why—they couldn't feel a thing—but he did all he could to please His Honor. He was anxious for the old man to ride back to his saloon and store and get the hell out of their lives.

"Dear Lord, we are gathered here today…."

Heads bowed, Andrew shared an impatient frown with Jackson as Watkins droned on and on. Obviously, the old man never suspected a thing about his oration being too long, 'cause he used the ceremony to speak on several things from saving their souls to the Lord showing mercy on the two orphans.

There in the dying day, the wind ruffled the pages of Watkins's Bible as he rambled some more. Andrew had not even considered himself and Jackson as orphans. They *were* orphans. Not that it mattered that much—just another day in Texas was all he'd called it. But they sure weren't past the judge's insistence about them having a guardian. That stuck in his craw. With the Pa gone, he knew they weren't going to accept a second boss if they could help it.

"Amen." Watkins slapped his top hat on his leg.

"Amen."

"What's for supper?" Watkins asked.

"Oatmeal," Jackson said.

"Sounds wonderful."

"Good." The boy turned on his heels and left.

"Where you——" The judge reached out.

Andrew caught Watkins's arm to stop him. "He'll be fine. Needs some time alone. Come on. I'll make us some supper."

"But—— but—— the grave needs covered."

"They ain't going nowhere. I'll do it later."

"That boy all right?" Watkins looked off in the twilight where Jackson had disappeared around the corral.

"Guess if you'd lost your ma and pa, you'd need some time alone, too."

"I'd probably need some whiskey. Your pa have any around here, maybe?"

It was an effort for Andrew not to roll his eyes. "I'll find some later. Let me get the water boiling for the oatmeal."

Watkins wiped his mouth on the back of his hand and looked once more in the direction Jackson went. Then he turned back and fell in with Andrew going to the house. "I hope he comes out of this all right."

"He will in time." Andrew lit a candle lamp on the table and then stoked the sheet-iron stove with mesquite-stick firewood. In minutes he had the fire going.

Satisfied, he closed the firebox door and turned as Jackson burst in the open door. "Damn Comanches——"

"What?" Watkins bolted from his upright nap in the chair.

"Injuns," Andrew said softly, picking up the muzzle-loading shotgun and going to the doorway. "Douse the light."

"What else do we need to do?" Watkins was already on his hands and knees on the floor by the table. Jackson half fell over him trying to blow out the flame on the candle.

"How many are there?" Andrew asked in soft whisper.

"Three or four."

"Bucks or boys?"

"What the hell difference does it make?" Watkins's voice squeaked. "Injuns are Injuns."

"Makes a helluva lot," Jackson hissed back. "Boys just hack around. Warriors come to kill ya."

"Which one?" Andrew asked his brother. The oil-smelling double barrel shotgun was heavy in his sweaty hands.

"I think they're boys."

"Good. You've got the forty-four loaded?"

"Yes."

"Get ready to use it."

"You two boys ain't taking on them Injuns?" Watkins's high-pitched voice squeaked in disbelief.

"Hush up. They'll hear you. There ain't time to talk about it." Andrew slipped outside.

Under the starlight, he knew from the uneasy horses that the raiders were in the corral. Watkins's burro was having a kicking, braying fit.

"Get your hands up!" Andrew ordered, running for the pen. From the corner of his eye, he saw Jackson with their Pa's pistol in his hand go to the left.

Dark figures went over the corral back fence like squirrels. Andrew ran faster to circle the pens. This was like the way Pa did it. His breath raged in an out. Those damn horse thieves would learn to leave Franks stock alone.

The bass crump of the .44 blasting away cut through the night. A horse screamed and a lithe figure jumped on a pony. Andrew plowed to stop, raised the shotgun to his shoulder, and fired. The rider fell off and the horse—also struck by the pellets— went bucking away.

"How many of them are there?"

"Three, and we got 'em all."

"Saddle a horse and catch theirs." Andrew walked slow-like toward the one on the ground that he'd shot.

"I will. We done it without Pa this time, didn't we? Didn't we?" Jackson huffed for his breath.

"Yeah, we did it without him." Andrew swallowed as he knelt beside the near-naked body and felt for his pulse. The Comanche stunk. Must have used old bear grease on his hair.

He was dead.

Watkins staggered around in disbelief like a drunken man in the starlight. "Oh, dear God, are these Indians all dead?" "If they ain't they will be," Andrew said.

"One—two—" Watkins beat his hat against his leg counting the corpses

"There's three of them,"

"You—you boys ever killed any Injuns before?"

"Yeah." Jackson handed Andrew the pistol. "I'll get a horse before theirs get away."

Watkins whirled. "Get away? What does he mean?"

Andrew shoved the pistol in his belt. "Those ponies will go home if we let 'em loose, and the tribe would send bucks back here right after them."

"So—so, what do you do with 'em?"

"Pa always sold 'em."

Watkins scratched his thin white hair. "I always wondered where he got them ponies."

One of the Indians moaned. Andrew shoved the shotgun in the judge's hands, walked over to the prone body, drew the Colt, cocked the hammer, aimed at the back of Comanche's head, and fired. The report rang out across the cedars and live oak

"Oh, my dear God!" Watkins moaned.

The work wasn't over yet. Now the boys had three *more* damn bodies to bury.

Been the same as if Pa was there, except this time they didn't need to listen to his harping the whole damn time about how slow they were.

"Where you going now?" Watkins asked, trying to keep up with Andrew.

"I've got oatmeal to cook."

"Yeah, yeah," Watkins said, looking back and then taking a double step or two to stay beside him.

"This court business over?" Andrew asked.

"Yeah, sure—but he don't have a gun. I mean your brother. He's going after those horses in the dark." Watkins talked away like he was in some kinda fog.

"Trust me. Jackson can see better in night than most folks can see in the daylight."

"But there could be more of them out there."

"He's just going after their horses."

Collapsed in a chair, the judge looked pale as a ghost when Andrew lit a candle on the table. He knew what the man needed and walked over to the trunk. Under some quilts he found a half-full bottle of Pa's whiskey, came back and set it on the table.

"I ain't got a glass."

Watkins waved off his concern, popped the cork out, and took a swig from the neck. Then in a voice cut by the liquor said, "Dear Jesus, I don't know about you two boys."

"I can tell you one thing. Me and Jackson are keeping this ranch. Ain't no blanket-ass Injuns or Texas law taking it away from us. We've worked hard on this place and the stock. We ain't being sent to no damn orphanage nor put in no one's home to be their slave."

Watkins dropped his head in defeat. "I understand. I understand. I promise."

Andrew stirred the oats into the boiling water. His heart beat so hard it hurt him deep inside. The judge damn well *better* understand him. The Franks brothers were staying on the

Turkey Track and neither hell nor high water nor Texas law was rooting them out.

By lantern, the boys buried the three dead Comanche boys in a common grave dug in the horse corrals. Hooves would soon disguise their dirt work, so even if their tracks might point there, any relatives came for the youths would find nothing. They only took a few hours' sleep. At last on his back listening to the night, Andrew knew things would be damn different from there on. But he had no idea how that would be.

FOUR

THE NEXT MORNING, Watkins took the three Comanche ponies back to town with him to sell. The spotted horses were tied head-to-tail and led about as well as his burro rode.

Before the JP left, he told the boys he'd have to study the law some more about their fate. He also carried in his pocket a list of what relatives the boys could recall from back in Arkansas he might be able to contact about their guardianship.

Andrew shut off his brother's angry protests and nodded to Watkins. "We'll see how it goes."

"I'll put the sale of these bangtails on your ledger at the store as credit."

"Fine." Andrew folded his arms over his chest, wary that Jackson might make another outburst.

When Watkins rode over the ridge, Andrew finally turned back to his brother. "We can't sleep here anymore."

"Huh?"

"I don't trust Watkins. He may find something in the law gives him authority over us."

"What're we going to do?"

"Sleep in the brush. Move around a lot."

"But what about the place?" Jackson gestured at the small house and grounds.

"We can keep it up. We just can't sleep here or let down our guard."

Jackson nodded slowly, like he was digesting the words. "Fer how long do you think?"

"Until we're old enough, I guess. We've got us a brand and some cattle. We need to catch some more. When we're old enough, they won't be able to bother us."

"We'll need some supplies sometime, won't we?"

"Maybe we can hire us someone to go in and get them for us."

"That's an idea. Andrew, we're going to live like Gawdamn outlaws, ain't we?"

Biting on his lower lip, Andrew nodded. His eyes hurt from looking so hard at the distant horizon. They'd be outlaws, all right. But they'd damn sure do what the situation called for them to exist.

They put things up and nailed the house door shut. Andrew wrote a note in pencil on the back of a calendar he tacked on the door.

This is property of the Franks Brothers. Any trespassers will be treated as our enemies. You can leave a note if you wish to contact us.

Jackson and Andrew Franks

Then, taking six horses—two loaded with packsaddles and two extras to ride on leads—they left the home place. Andrew knew Jackson was as close to crying as at any time in the past few days. A knot behind his own tongue could not be swallowed. He booted the pony he called Tob—a slender bay gelding—and headed west.

"We going to Swain Creek?"

Andrew nodded. "Good place to catch some cattle, I think."

The creek had some good water holes, and a few they'd fixed using cypress boxes they sunk in the water bearing sand that filled with liquid. There were a few cottonwoods for shade. Andrew always wondered why his pa didn't make his claim out there. He'd never bothered to ask him why, though. Any question like that Pa would have been considered an offensive challenge to his authority.

They set up camp in late afternoon, then rustled up some sticks and dry chips for firewood. Jackson hung out a tarp for shade and shelter over their panniers and bedrolls while Andrew cooked them some oats. They ate as the sun set.

Jackson sat cross-legged on the other side of the fire, eating slow to make it last. "What're we doing tomorrow?"

"Catching and yoking some steers. We need to do lots of that."

"What're they worth, anyway?"

"The war'll be over someday. Pa figured it ever got over, folks would need beef."

"Why, there's plenty of hawgs just for the gathering. Who'd want an old tough steer to eat?"

Andrew wasn't going to argue. If all they did was sell a hide off their steers, it would beat nothing. They needed to brand lots of them. Besides, being busy would take lots of things off their minds— they needed that too, being busy.

Sunup, they were in the saddle and shaking their riatas out. Some slick-eared cattle had moseyed down on the creek the evening before. They'd heard them bawl in the night and Jackson snuck up to look them over. He came back excited.

"There's several in the bunch. No earmarks, so they must be unbranded."

"Good, we'll put them in the tally book."

"You got it, huh? The one Pa had?"

"Sure. A man's got a ranch needs a tally book."

Jackson bobbed his head. "We don't really need Pa giving us orders to do this, do we?"

"We handled them Comanche like he did."

"Yeah. Here's to catching cattle." Jackson gave him a stiff nod. "The Franks Brothers are adding cattle to the tally book today."

They rode out that morning when the live oak, cedar, and pancake cactus beds rested under a soft purple light. The cattle looked like stick figures when they discovered them and took off in a hard trot. The boys soon closed in on them. Jackson swung his rope out and caught half a face and a horn on the nearest yearling, dallied his lariat on the horn, and then charged his horse past the critter, tossed the slack over the black yearling's back, and rolled his dun sideways.

The longhorn went down in a great flip. Andrew rode up, dismounted, and tied three feet together before he could recover. He undid Jackson's rope and tossed it free so he could recoil it. A nod and they were off again. The older ones were long gone, but another yearling had lagged back. He'd regret it.

In a few minutes they were chousing the laggard one. Jackson in the lead, Andrew made sure the yearling didn't veer off. The rope hissed through the air and caught the unmarked one around the stubby horns. Jackson dallied his rope on the horn, rode past the animal, tossed the slack over him, and then went left. His moves upended the dark brown yearling, Andrew rode up, dismounted, and three-legged tied him before he got his breath back.

"Two more for the Turkey Track." On foot, Jackson walked over, busy coiling his rope. "You know in a year we'd have over seven hundred head branded if every day went this well."

"They won't," Andrew promised him. "Build a fire. We need them branded and worked."

"Ah, mountain oysters. I can hardly wait."

"Well, they won't get cooked 'less we have a fire."

"All right—Pa. Hell, we're working for ourselves now."

Andrew looked up from stroking his jackknife blade over a whetstone to put a better edge on it. "That means there's only two of us. Means we've got to do his job too."

"Hell." Jackson laughed. "You can do the thinking and work, too, can't you?"

Ready to bend over and notch the yearling's left ear, Andrew looked up at his brother and smiled. He was right. Soon laughter consumed him, too. They were their own bosses. Pa never did nothing, anyway, but set a horse and let them do it all. It was funny.

The job completed, Andrew finally closed his jackknife and slipped it back in his pocket. He staggered over consumed in laughter and put a hand on Jackson's shoulder.

"You—" Choked with laughter, Jackson had to stop to talk. "You can do that good as he could and work—can't you?"

"I— I think so." Tears soon clouded Andrew's vision. He felt a pain in his chest and it rose in his throat like a big knot. "Damn him, anyway. Gawdamn him for doing that to Ma."

Sober faced, Jackson clapped him on the shoulders. "I'll never miss him. But Andrew, I miss her. I even hurt thinking how she'll never be there again when we go in."

The wind rose. At last Andrew gave him a nod, snuffed his nose, and went to start the fire. Their bawling yearling was ear-notched, his large scrotum cut open and his seeds removed. Andrew tossed the first ones on the fire heating the branding iron.

"First one pops out of the fire is yours."

In a short while it popped out of the fire. Jackson ran over and stabbed the treasure with his jackknife. He brushed off some of the grit with the back of his fingers and then bit off a chunk. A smile crossed his face and he gave his brother a nod of approval.

"Best damn oysters I've had in ages."

"Ah, hell you was just starved for something besides oatmeal." Andrew went after his own trophy.

After his first bite he agreed with his twin. The sweet meat drew saliva in his mouth in a flood. Finished branding number one, they worked the other one, then yoked those two together. Once yoked together, the steers became all tangled up and fell down in their new fix. It kept the boys laughing as they rode back to camp.

Andrew stripped out the latigo leathers to unsaddle his horse.

"Ain't no way we can catch seven hundred steers." "Why?"

"We only got twelve yokes— Hey, grab the shotgun, we've got company coming."

"Huh?" Three riders were headed their way, about two hundred yards away and closing quickly. Jackson whirled, gulped, then obeyed his brother's order.

Andrew drew his reloaded cap-and-ball .44 out of his saddlebags and held it by the side of his leg. The riders wore hats. Not Indians. He looked closer. Two were Mexicans. The one in the center wore a felt hat.

They reined up about thirty feet away. The bearded gringo in the center was Jack McCory. He ran an outfit east of them, the JM brand. A burly man near forty, the two Mexican *vaqueros* looked like they were there to back him.

McCory slapped his saddle horn with his gloved hand. "So I heard the old man shot hisself and your Ma."

Andrew shrugged. "So?"

"You boys acting hostile to me?"

"State your business then."

A sly grin parted McCory's beard covered mouth. "Listen, you boys wouldn't stand a chance against me and these *companeros*." He used a thumb to indicate the two hard-eyed Mexicans.

Jackson gestured with the barrel of his shotgun. "Comes to cut and shoot mister, this old scattergun will get at least two of you. Maybe all three."

McCory held up his hands. "I come to offer you boys fifty bucks for your place."

Andrew snorted. "Ride on."

"I said I—" The sound of Jackson snapping the ears back on the shotgun cut off McCory's words. "Listen to me—"

"Our conversation is over." Andrew waved the pistol for them to clear out.

McCory gritted his teeth. "You're going to damn sure regret this. I guarantee it."

"We've been regretting a lot lately, but it won't be running your ass off."

"You dumb boys'll come beg me to buy you out."

"Get out of here!" Jackson screamed and stepped toward them menacing the scattergun as they hurriedly spun their horses around and left. He watched them go, fading into the dusk. He looked over at his brother. "Figure they'll be back?"

"He ain't one that understands the word no." Andrew shook his head, chewing thoughtfully on his lower lip. They'd have to be on their guard day and night from now on.

—

A WEEK PASSED. They had all their yokes on cattle and felt good enough about their success to take a bath in the knee-deep water hole in the creek under the rustling cottonwoods. Their thread-bare, freshly-washed clothing hung on some mesquite bushes to dry, and the two naked boys used the sandy mud to scrub their bodies with.

Jackson washed the last traces of dirt out of his hair. "Where we going to get more yokes?"

"There's those Mexicans at San Juan where Pa got them."

"How much will they want for them?"

"Maybe twenty cents apiece."

"You got the money. How many can we buy?"

"Oh, enough for now."

Jackson waded out of the pool and dripping off, looked back. "It'd be nice to see someone besides ourselves for a change."

Andrew finished up rinsing off. A break in their cow-catching wouldn't hurt at all. Besides, those friendly Mexican people at the small community shouldn't be a threat to them.

They turned in at sundown with plans to get up before dawn and head for San Juan. Andrew fell asleep to the cries of a coyote out in the greasewood and the rustle of the night wind through the cottonwoods overhead.

Sound asleep, he never knew what first hit him.

It felt like a bull had gored him in the side. By the time he got turned over, he was awake enough to realize he was being kicked, instead—over and over, in his head, side, and belly.

He managed to get his head out from under the blanket. In the faint glow of starlight, he caught sight of a familiar hat right before another boot toe drove the wind out of him.

"You boys better learn, you threaten me, I'll make a believer out of you two little pissants."

McCory.

Then the lights went out.

"Andrew? Andrew? You alive?"

He blinked—or tried to, at least. His eyes were so swollen, they'd barely open. He worked his mouth around, felt a couple of loose teeth and a busted lip.

Andrew spat. "Take more than Jack McCory to kill me."

"They run off our hosses—cut our girths, pissed on our food and—and took our guns."

Andrew sat up and held his pounding head. "They're going to wish they'd killed us."

"They break anything?"

"My ribs, I guess." The catch in his side felt like the time a bronc had piled him in a ball. He met Jackson's gaze. "I look as bad as you do?"

"Maybe worse."

Andrew nodded. He owed Jack McCory a beating he wouldn't forget. Maybe he'd even kill the sumbitch.

"How did they get to us?"

"We let our guard down. It won't happen again." Andrew closed his sore eyes against the glare from the early morning sun. "Stayed here in one place so long that they had us spotted."

"What're we going to do? We ain't got no horses. No saddles—I mean no cinches."

"There's some cinches at the home place. One of those horses will come back. One of us can ride over there."

"What about food?"

"I hurt too damn bad to even think about it." Andrew laid back down, tried to close his eyes and escape the pain.

He must have fallen asleep. It was near sundown when he awoke again and couldn't find Jackson. His vision was fuzzy when he sat up to look for his twin and he hurt in every direction. His lower lip was split and some cut above his right eye had leaked blood down over his face, because his right eyelashes were matted shut. He'd been beat before by Pa but McCory had a worse handle on it than their pa'd ever had.

"Andrew. Andrew!" Jackson's voice brought him awake to the world of pain again. This time the stars were above him.

"What?"

"Oh, thank God." His twin was on his knees hovering over him. "I got three horses. The others will come in. Got the girths and some food from the ranch."

"Good."

"I'll make us some corn mush."

"Sure. Didn't see any one?"

"No, but we got a letter."

"Where did you find that?' Andrew sat up and tried to see who it was from in the dark.

"Hold up. I brung a candle. I figured it'd be dark by the time I got back here."

Andrew sat back and waited, his breath coming in short wheezes. At last, Jackson got the candle lit, and he opened the envelope and turned the page.

Dear Andrew and Jackson,

I received a letter recently from a Judge Watkins of Los Olivos, Texas who said I was needed at your ranch, since both your parents had passed away. Being a cousin to your mother, the judge felt I was the nearest kin to be your guardian. My own husband, Farley, unfortunately was killed in wagon wreck a few months ago so I know about losses of loved ones.

I plan to arrive at this Los Olivos Saloon and Store on the fifteenth of June. I hope you can meet me there. If not, I will await your arrival to escort me to the ranch.

Sincerely yours,
Sophie Grenada

Andrew handed the letter to his brother and shook his sore head in disgust. All they needed was some busybody old woman. In the midst of a range war with McCory, now they'd have to deal with her coming to run their business thanks to Judge Watkins.

"What's the date today?" Jackson asked.

"How should I know?" Andrew laid back down. He hurt too bad to think.

"Here." Jackson bent over him with a tablespoon and some medicine. "Laudanum. It'll help the pain then I'll cook the mush."

"I don't—"

"You're getting it, anyway. Even if I have to hold your nose and shove it down your throat."

He braced himself and rose up. The medicine tasted bitter

and he glared at his brother for making him take it. There was not a muscle in his body that didn't scream at him.

Jackson shook him awake again sometime later. "Here eat some of this mush."

Andrew moaned and turned away. He didn't care. He didn't care about anything. The pain was gone. He felt limber-necked. What did Jackson want anyway? Just let him sleep.

FIVE

AT A GOOD distance, they sat their horses and watched the road from Mason. For two days they had thought it was the fifteenth of the month. This had to be the day. Then the dust of the mail buckboard boiled up in the sky. Sitting beside the driver on the spring seat was a woman wearing a straw hat. They turned and nodded to each other.

Cousin Sophie had arrived.

Jackson looked disgusted. He shook his head. "So what now? We still ain't got a gun between us."

"I know, I know. We've waited this long." Andrew shrugged. "I guess since the judge ordered her here, it'll be safe enough to ride in and get her."

"But she—I mean what if'n she thinks we've got a big ranch?"

"You're meaning we ain't got a fancy place?"

"Yes."

"Well, then, the sooner she'll leave us alone."

"You mean go back where she come from?"

"Amen."

But even as he said it, Andrew couldn't believe it. If she did leave, she'd want to take them along, being their guardian. And they sure as hell weren't leaving the Turkey Track. Not cause of McCory, or this Cousin Sophie.

They rode slowly up to the store and saloon, leading a saddle horse for her and a packhorse in case she had trunks. While thinking about the implications of this woman's arrival, Andrew made up his mind on another matter. They needed two revolvers, at least one, and it was time to get them. No telling when they'd run into McCory again.

On the windswept porch of the store, an ample-hipped woman stood beside her leather trunk. The breeze tugged at her blue dress enough to show her petticoats, and she held a straw hat on to keep from losing it. The driver accepted her money for the fare and with clear blue eyes she looked hard at the two of them.

"You Jackson and Andrew?"

"Yes ma'am." Andrew took off his hat and gave a small bow. "Jackson'll load your things. I have to go inside and buy something."

"Do I need to talk to the judge?" She searched around, but there was no one around but them.

Andrew shrugged. "Can if you want." He mounted the stairs and went inside the store. His stomach was full of the worms of dread over the denial he expected.

A boy in an apron close to his age asked if he could help him. Said his name was Tad.

"You have two forty-four Colts?"

"New or used?"

"I have credit—name's Franks."

"I'll look. The judge ain't here right now."

Good, she wouldn't get to talk to him.

Tad went to the ledger book. "You Andrew or Jackson?"

"Andrew. Jackson's my twin brother."

"Says here that you have eighteen dollars of credit."

Andrew squinted in pain at the figure. "That's all them Injun ponies brung?"

The boy shrugged.

"Will that buy two used forty-fours?"

"Sure."

"Let me see them."

The boy reached in and began to place on the counter several Navy-model Colts in old cracked leather holsters and belts.

"How are they priced?"

"Five dollars for most of them. One or two are like new. They cost seven-fifty."

"Which ones are the new ones?" Newer firearms would be better if they could afford them.

The clerk searched them out and unsheathed the first one. It was in better condition than the one McCory stole. The second gun was in similar shape.

"I'll take them. How much is a double-barrel shotgun?" He indicated the rack behind the counter.

"Oh, ten bucks."

Andrew made a face and pounded the counter with his fist. Too much, they couldn't afford one of them.

"How much do you need?"

He whirled and found his newly-arrived guardian standing behind him. She'd heard the whole conversation. Andrew swallowed, and met her gaze, decided to take a chance. "I only have three dollars credit left, and they cost ten.

She reached down inside her dress front and produced a stack of bills. "I have seven dollars."

"You don't have to do this."

"Jackson said they stole your weapons. I can handle a shotgun." She counted out the money and pushed it at the young clerk. "You boys have any coffee out there?"

"No ma'am." Pa never would let their mother buy it—it had cost too much.

Sophie nodded to the clerk. "Two pounds of Arbuckle."

"Yes, ma'am."

She looked back at Andrew. "Anything else?"

"We could use fifty pounds of rolled oats."

A frown spread over her face. "What else're we going to eat?"

He shrugged. "Oatmeal's all I know how to fix. Ma done all the cooking 'fore she and Pa died."

"What all can we get on that pony out there?"

"He's stout."

She nodded and spoke up again. "Young man, I want a sack of flour, baking powder—a big can—some raisins, dried apples, five pounds of bacon, ten pounds of sugar, and ten air-tight peaches and tomatoes."

With a sharp nod for Andrew and a wink, she smiled. "Variety isn't bad. Oh, and fifty pounds of pinto beans. One of us can carry that over our laps, huh?"

"Um—uh-huh." Andrew nodded lamely. He couldn't think of another thing to say. This woman was not at all what he'd expected.

It had always seemed like his mother had just gotten along to get along, letting Pa ride roughshod over her to make all the decisions. It was already obvious that Sophie was nothing like that. She had no problem making decisions, and she did so quickly, and with confidence. And while she was definitely the take-charge type, she hadn't batted an eyelash at his purchase of the pistols, even chipping in extra to buy the shotgun.

"Why don't you go give your brother his pistol and tell him to make some more room on the horses for our supplies?"

"Yes, ma'am." Grabbing up his new pistol, he strapped it on, adjusting where it sat on his leg while avoiding her eyes. Then he snagged Jackson's Colt off the counter and beat a hasty retreat out the front door. He was going to need some time to think about these new developments.

Jackson was outside, leaning against the boardwalk rail. Andrew caught his attention and tossed him the gun and belt set.

Jackson caught it and blinked. "What's she doing in there?"

"Paying for a shotgun. Let's get these hog legs loaded."

"Amen, I've been plumb nervous for days that we'd meet up with McCory and them gunnies again and be unarmed." Jackson gave a great exhale. He hopped down the steps to his horse and took caps, powder, and bullets out of his saddlebags.

Sophie came out and sat down on the porch edge while they loaded the new revolvers. For several minutes she didn't say a word, just sat there with her head down swinging her legs lazily back and forth.

"So someone stole your guns?" She kept her gaze on her swinging shoes, not even bothering to look up. "Were those the same ones beat the billy-be-damn out of you two?"

Shocked at her language, Andrew frowned. "His name's McCory. Him and two of his *vaqueros* caught us asleep."

"Guess he needs a lesson or two."

Jackson looked up from his work of ramming powder and balls in the cylinders. "That's what we aimed to give him. Right between his eyes—*bang*."

She shook her head. "Naw, there's better ways than that."

"What's that?"

"A snake in his saddlebags. A dead critter in his well bucket." She stopped pumping her feet and stood. "There's more ways to skinning a cat than to cut his head off."

The clerk came out the door with all of their purchases piled on a handcart. Andrew stifled a laugh as Jackson's eyes flew open at the sight it all.

"Now we'll have to hold some of it on our laps," Sophie cautioned. "That poor packhorse can't carry it all."

"Yes ma'am." For maybe the first time in his life, Jackson had no argument to offer, and immediately began loading the packhorse When they rode away a few minutes later, he shook his head in wonder. "Pa'd never bought that much in five years."

Sophie threw her head back and laughed out loud. "Good thing he ain't here, then."

Andrew couldn't help but chuckle. Sophie was really unlike any woman he'd ever known. She didn't ride side-saddle, either, all prim and proper like some snotty woman from the city. She rode astride, with her straw hat tied on, ignoring the wind whipping around her head, with the tail end of her white petticoats exposed. While her nose and mouth were too big to be called beautiful, her smile was infectious, and her dark eyes bright and captivating.

"So what've you boys been doing out here all on your own?"

"Catching cattle and branding them."

"What you're going to do with 'em?"

The sack of pinto beans was slung over Jackson's legs. He re-balanced it gingerly, then gave her a shy smile. "Sell 'em for hides, if nothing else."

"Oh, there'll be slaughterhouses will need them somewhere. You boys are doing the right thing."

Andrew's chest swelled with pride. "Pa had over a hundred cows branded and in his tally book to make us a herd of our own. Lately we been singling out wild yearlings and yoking them. But we need more yokes."

"Where do you get them?"

He winced. "Before we were attacked, we were going to a place named San Juan to get some more yokes."

She gave a nod of approval. "And they cost what?"

"Twenty cents apiece."

"How many you need?"

"Oh, a couple dozen."

"How will we get them up here?"

"Last time an old Mexican brought them out to the ranch on an ox cart for twenty-five cents."

She twisted to look back across the knee-high grass and

prickly pear beds and then she turned to the front. "We better go get those yokes and get busy."

Andrew nodded. "We can go in a day, huh?"

"Sure." Jackson perked up again. "But — well, why are you doing all this for us?"

Andrew rolled his eyes. He knew what came next. "Damn it, Jackson — "

Sophie grinned and held up a hand. "No, no, Andrew. I don't mind him asking." She turned back to Jackson. "My husband was killed in a wagon wreck a while back, so I sold our farm. It didn't bring that much 'cause of the war still being on, but I'm here with y'all till you run me off."

"Oh." Jackson stopped, his face turning red. "Well, uh — I mean, you're not what we thought at all. We ain't going to run you off, Sophie."

She reached over, grasped his arm, and shook him in the saddle. "Don't say that yet, you ain't seen my bad side."

They all laughed at that, and just like that the ice was broken.

It didn't take all that long for them to reach the old homestead. They found it more or less as they'd left it — a sad little house built of posts and timber and a canvas roof. Sophie appraised it with a keen glance and gave a little nod.

"It sure ain't no palace, and it needs some fixing for sure. Let me tell you, though — I've seen worse."

With that, she set about putting things in order. She was no stranger to keeping house, and it showed. While the boys rushed around putting away supplies in the places she told them, Sophie swept out and cleaned the little kitchen with ruthless efficiency. By the time she started dinner — biscuits and gravy — it was cleaner than Jackson and Andrew had ever seen it.

Talk about a new broom sweeping clean.

Sophie used a biscuit to sop up the leftover gravy on her plate. "So them galoots got your money, guns, and what else?"

"They, ah—peed in our oats too."

"Doing that deserves a mean trick. By the way, how much salt you two rub in that pork you cured?"

Andrew swallowed a moutful of his dinner. "Is it ruined?"

"No, but I'll have to soak it a day to ever use it." She laughed. "In Arkansas, we shot wild game. What's around here?"

"I—" Jackson stopped, another forkful halfway to his lips. He cocked his head. "Do you hear that?"

"Hear what?"

He bolted for the door. "Something's in our horses."

Andrew leaned forward and blew out the candles. He turned to Sophie. "Keep that shotgun handy."

"I will," she said in a hushed voice.

Their new Colts were hung by their belts and holsters on pegs up on the wall. Creeping across the wood floor on tiptoes, the boys pulled the guns before moving out the door and into the night full of creaking insects.

Snorting and prancing in the corral, the horses were clearly upset with something. Andrew waved for Jackson to go west of the pens while he started for the right side. Whoever it was, they couldn't get the horses out the backside unless they unstacked the poles—too much work for horse thieves.

Reaching the fence, Andrew cocked his piece and sucked in a deep breath. "Get your hands in the air!"

"Don't shoot, *señor.* Don't shoot!"

That wasn't the response he'd expected. "Come over to the gate. How many of you are there?"

"Just me."

"Jackson, get in there and check it out."

"You got it."

A short little Mexican man appeared in the dark, hands held high in the air. Andrew waved him over with the pistol. "You get out here. What in hell were you doing in our horse lot?"

"Nothing, *señor*. I am a poor man trying to get home."

"Yeah and you were going to steal a horse, weren't you?" He closed the gate and hooked the loop over the top.

Jackson climbed over the fence. "It's okay now, Sophie. We've got him."

"Who is it?"

Andrew nudged their new "guest." "What's your name?"

"Pinto Palo."

"What're you doing in this country?"

"*Señor*, I only want to go home. My little ones I have not seen in many months, and ah, my wife Margarita. I have walked many miles and hoped to borrow a burro."

"Steal one you mean?"

"Oh, *señor*, I would only borrow it."

"Where's your family?"

"Chihuahua."

Sophie joined them from the house. "What was he doing?"

Jackson rolled his eyes and dropped his pistol. "He says he was borrowing a burro."

"What would you do with a burro?"

"Ah, *señora*, I could never ride a horse." He shrugged, his arms still raised, eyeing Andrew's pistol warily. "They are far too tall for a man of my size."

Sophie reached over and pushed the barrel of the gun down to point at the ground. "What've you been doing up here?"

The little man sighed in relief and lowered his arms. "Making adobe blocks in San Antonio, *señora*."

"How much do they pay you?"

"Ah, *señora*, they pay me ten cents a day. They are very cheap people, this man I work for."

"Can you lay bricks, too?"

"Oh, *sí*, I can build *castles*." He brightened, threw his hands back up at the sky to show how tall they'd be.

She smiled and waved toward the house. "Come sit with us, *Señor* Palo. Let's talk."

"Oh, *si, señora*." He grinned, displaying a mouthful of stained and broken teeth. "It will be my pleasure."

Andrew touched her arm. "What are you doing?"

"Can we loan him a mount?"

He looked at her incredulously. "You think he'll come back?"

She nodded toward the house. "Some people are worth taking chances on."

He chewed on that for a moment, then saw just where it was she was going with this. With a chuckle, he let the hammer on the Colt down, spun the cylinder to an empty one, and stuck it in the waistband of his britches. "We've got some burros Jackson and I rode when we were younger. They're out in another pen not far from here."

She gave him a wink then turned back to their visitor. "*Señor* Palo, I have an offer for you."

"Oh, *gracias. Madre de Dias*, I swear I would never steal a horse."

"These boys will get you a burro to ride home in the morning, but you must return in thirty days and work for me. I pay twenty-five cents a day."

"Doing what, may I ask, *señora*?"

"Building an adobe house for us."

He nodded, then surprised them by taking off his hat and sweeping the ground with it in a deep bow. "I would be honored."

Jackson shook his head and snorted. "I've seen it all now. We catch a horse thief and she makes a deal for him to come back and build her a house."

Andrew slugged him in the arm. "Shut it, Jackson."

Ignoring the remark, Sophie took Palo by the arm and ushered him toward the house. "Come on. I have some food left over for you. "

"Oh, *gracias, señora*." He fell in behind her like a puppy dog.

Jackson caught his brother by the sleeve as they disappeared into the house. "She sure is different. Different as hell."

"Hell's what we've been used to, brother. She'll sure do."

Jackson opened the door and went in. For his part, Andrew stood and listened to the coyotes for a moment, then he too went inside. As he did, he realized for once he sure didn't dread crossing that threshold.

That was different as hell, all right.

SIX

PINTO PALO RODE out the next morning on Jed, Jackson's old burro. In an ancient saddle they'd fixed for him, he left still thanking Sophie and telling her he would be back to build her a *grandé hacienda*.

Jackson's mood hadn't improved overnight. "He never thanked us a time for not hanging his turkey neck. Bet I don't see that damn burro ever again, either."

Andrew chuckled. "You hate that burro. We didn't have horses back then and we had to ride them pokey things after Pa's horse."

"Yeah, well, I still hate them."

"We better get that packhorse loaded if we still plan on going to San Juan today."

His brother's voice turned quiet. "Do you know what she plans on using for a bedroll?"

"No." Andrew's eyebrows went up. "Why?"

"Well, we just sleep on any old blanket on the ground." He kept looking back toward the house to see if she was coming.

"I better ask her."

Jackson sighed in relief. "I didn't know much about Ma, and I sure don't know much about her."

"Lots that neither of us know about women."

The other boy looked particularly uncomfortable. "Makes my skin crawl at times."

"Yeah. I'll go ask her."

He met Sophie coming out the door. "Jackson and me, we just sleep on the ground—I mean we ain't got a bed for you."

She looked rather serious at him. "Then I'll go get a blanket." She started to turn back inside.

"Sophie?"

"Yes?" She stopped, turned back, and swept the hair from her face. "Everything okay?"

"Well, me and Jackson don't know half the ways of a—well, of a woman. See, Ma never rode nowhere with us. She always stayed here and tended things. Jackson and me and Pa went out there for several days wherever the unmarked cattle were at."

"And you're worried having a woman along is going to cramp you two?"

"I guess."

"I reckon you by now figured I ain't no house pet. Sure get bored quick at that. So we'll figure out how to make each other comfortable out there. Fair enough?"

"Sure."

"Good, I'll get me a bedroll." She ducked back and went inside.

He walked back over to where Jackson sat. "You hear her?"

"I hope so. My lands, she's going with us cow hunting?"

Andrew laughed. "I think it'll improve our meals."

Jackson scrambled up at the sight of her coming and brushed off his seat. "She's already done that."

The sun was low in the west when they watered their horses at the San Juan village well in the center of the square. The cool well water they drew up cut the trail dust of the day while their mounts slobbered in the trough.

Andrew recalled their previous visit here, when they'd ridden over to buy the first set of yokes. Pa had left them in their camp overnight while he'd gone to the *cantina*, drank *mescal*, and messed with the "women" who worked in there. The next morning he'd showed out to the camp at sunup, hung over as a bear that had been hibernating all winter, cussing them for not having breakfast ready.

It wasn't the lecture that he remembered the most, though. It was the perfume he'd smelled all over the old man.

Later that morning, the three of them had been watering their horses at the well and trough when a brown-skinned women hardly older than the twins had sauntered down the street and fawned all over Pa. Andrew had been embarrassed to see his own father pull her close and squeeze her butt with such familiarity. But after their brief tryst, he'd known the source of the flowery perfume.

Sophie's voice pulled him out of his thoughts. "Where will we stay tonight, boys?"

Jackson tossed his head back the way they'd come. "Out in the desert. Where else?"

"It's late. Let me buy some food for us to eat."

"But we don't have——"

She cut him off. "How much could it really cost?"

"Well, how should I know?"

"*Señora!*" Sophie waved to a woman all wrapped in a blanket who was crossing the square. "Is there a food vendor here?"

"Ah, *sí, señora.*" She pointed to a house behind her.

"*Gracias.*" Sophie turned back to the twins. "Over at that doorway. The lighted one."

Jackson still sounded undecided. "What will they have to eat?"

"Who knows? Beef? Goat? It'll be fiery hot and rich." She threw her arm over his shoulder and herded him toward the indicated door, waving for Andrew to come, too.

The old woman made them each giant flour tortillas and cooked them on a black grill. Then she filled each one with a thick sauce of meat and beans. Rolled up into a burrito, she handed one to each of them and accepted Sophie's dime with a small smile.

The boys ate squatted in the gathering darkness at the old woman's doorway. Sophie sat on an old crate. She'd been right about the food.

She gave them a wink. "That's better than oatmeal, I'd say."

Andrew agreed, but he still felt uncomfortable about spending a dime on their meal. Too long he'd heard the old man say over and over again—waste not, want not. Then he wondered what the flower-smelling girl and all the liquor he'd drank that night had cost. Maybe Pa had had two plans—one for them and Ma, and another for himself.

Bastard.

Andrew didn't miss the old man at all. But damn sure the likes of McCory would never have attacked Pa in camp. McCory'd never lived through it.

Could he, Jackson, and Sophie stand up to someone like that?

When the music from the cantina filtered out in the street, Sophie looked at them with a smile. "Can you boys dance?"

"No, ma'am." Jackson wiped his mouth on the back of his hand. "Pa said dancing was the devil's business. He never wanted to catch us doing it either."

"He go to church regular?"

Jackson shook his head. "Lord, no."

"How'd he know so much about the devil's work then?"

Andrew chuckled. "Hell almighty, Sophie, he'd a' sure blown up at you for asking him that. Won't he, Jackson?"

"We wouldn't have dared." Jackson laughed and went over to face the horses like they were somebody. "Now, Pryor Franks, have I ever seen you in church?"

A horse in the line snorted in his face and made the bits ring on his teeth.

"I thought that. You never were in one. And oh, yes, you said the devil was in that little Catholic Church over there across the square, too. And if we ever went in there, we'd be struck down dead too, didn't you?"

"Sounds to me like you boys got the full course from him. The full course of horseshit, that is." She considered the last half of her large burrito. "Here, Jackson, finish this. I'm too full to eat another bite."

Nodding his thanks, he took the leftovers and tucked in. "We learned it all from him."

Andrew belched, long and loud. His face grew hot. "Sorry about that. After all this I need some water. Good food, but, boy, was it was hot."

"I met your pa one time when y'all were leaving Arkansas." Sophie stood to join them on the street and led the way back toward the well. "Y'all came by our place in Yell County. After that, I didn't care if I ever saw him again."

Andrew traded a quick glance with his brother. What had Pa done to her? There'd been something in her tone he'd never heard before—a strong bitterness that rang like a bell.

He tried to recall their harsh trip from Arkansas. It had been a miserable time for two twelve-year-old boys. The roads were rough and bad rutted. It had rained a lot. Cold drops like ice went through their thin clothing, soaking them to the skin while they struggled to keep the two wagons moving. Ma drove one and Pa drove the other. He'd whipped the teams constantly—and whipped them, too. Dry Texas was a paradise when they finally made it there.

But, try as he might, he couldn't recall their stopover at Sophie's parents' farm. Why not? Maybe like all those beatings, all those shakings Pa gave him, it had been absorbed into the mass of things he didn't want to remember.

She handed Andrew the gourd dipper. "Here, this'll chase some of that hot stuff."

Jackson nudged him, jerked his head toward the street. "Don't look now. But that guy just rode in was one of McCory's men."

"You sure?"

The younger boy didn't move a muscle. "Pretty sure."

The rider reined up outside the *cantina* and dismounted. As he slapped the trail dust from his clothes, one of the *cantina* girls ran outside and nearly tackled him.

"Ah, *mia Benito*! Where have you been for so long, my lover?"

"Ah, Carmella, let's go inside, my darling. I'm so thirsty."

Holding each other, they went in the swinging doors talking and laughing.

Jackson let out a long breath. "He never saw us."

"Good." Andrew wasn't sure how to proceed now. Was the man's appearance here—now—a coincidence? Or had McCory had him follow them here? Either way, they needed to be ready for any eventuality. "I think we better go make camp."

His brother nodded. "No argument here."

Sophie yelped and stepped away from something on the ground. "What is that?"

Jackson squatted and struck a match. Cupping it in his hand, he held it over a small mound in the dirt. "It's a dead kitten."

Andrew shuddered. The small cat's eyes had sunken in. It had been dead for some time.

Jackson scooped it up. Before Andrew could stop him, he stole his way over to the horse McCory's *vaquero* had just tied to the hitching post outside the *cantina*. He stuck the dead critter in the saddlebags, then hurried back to wash his hands in the trough.

His grin was huge as he dried his hands on his britches. "Bet he likes that real well in a hot day or two."

Shaking his head, Andrew mounted his own horse. He wasn't sure how the hardcase would take finding a dead cat in his saddlebags, but it did make him grin. At times, his brother could show a real mean streak in him.

When they rode out of the square in the darkness, Sophie looked back. "Now it's their turn to start worrying about who's out to get *them*."

Jackson sounded enthused. "That's the plan, ain't it?"

"Sure."

Andrew disagreed, but kept his peace for now. A dead critter in a saddlebag wasn't enough for him. Not by a long shot. What he really wanted was to stomp them all. He'd never forget waking up to a beating like that. Nothing would satisfy him until he took it out of McCory's fat ass—personally.

SEVEN

MCCORY'S MAN AND his horse were gone the next morning when they rode back into town. Without further incident, they found the carpenter who made his yokes from cottonwood and willow. His name was Paulo, and he showed them his wares with quiet pride.

Andrew looked them over. They were cruder-made and lighter than the walnut and oak harnesses he knew from the Ozarks, but they would work. "How many can we have now?"

"Two dozen, *señor*."

"How long before we can buy more?"

"I can have that many more in... maybe two weeks?"

He nodded. "And you can get them delivered to us for twenty-five cents?"

"*Si, señor*, but my man is slow."

"That's fine. We'll take some with us and have him bring the rest." Andrew stepped out of the little shop to speak to Sophie. "We owe him six dollars for the yokes he has now, plus another two dozen he'll make for us. Plus a quarter to deliver them."

She counted out the bills and they paid for their purchase. Paulo helped them load up their horses with the half-dozen harnesses they were taking back with them now, and then shook each of their hands in thanks.

By sundown, they were back at the ranch. Sophie hurried off to the house and the boys began pulling latigo leather loose, unsaddling and turning the horses out in the corral. In a log trough, Jackson rationed out some hard ear corn that came from a German farmer who lived near Mason. He noticed that the corn bin was getting low and reminded Andrew of it.

"We need to find a damn money tree. A wagonload of corn would cost us twenty dollars." Andrew tossed his saddle on the fence in disgust. "How did the old man do it?"

"He never spent no money."

"No, but he paid cash for that last load of corn."

"He sold them Comanche ponies we gathered."

Andrew shook his head. "No more than the ones we send in brought, they wouldn't pay for half a wagon of corn."

"He sold some pigs." Jackson shrugged, looking perplexed. "What can we do? Sophie's money won't last forever."

Andrew lugged her saddle over to the fence and swung it on top. "Wish to hell he'd talked more about how he did things like get money than bitching at us all the time."

Jackson reached over his head to stretch his arms and back. "Wasn't none of our damn business."

Andrew spat on the dusty ground. This was frustrating as hell. "That's what he thought, all right. We better get back to catching cattle."

"I'm ready when you are. Let's go see what's for supper."

Sophie had some biscuits and fried pork ready for them on the dining room table. They sat down as she poured three mugs of coffee and joined them. "How much money did McCory steal from you boys?"

"Pa had about seven dollars on him. We looked in his boots and all over. So it was seven dollars they took. Why?"

"How did Pryor ever stay here? I mean, you boys've lived here over five years. He never sold nothing much did he?"

Andrew opened a biscuit and the steam rose from it. "Jackson and I were discussing that earlier. We never knew about his money, but he had to have it to buy some food, saddles, ropes, salt, corn, and all the other things we need around here."

"Well, then, where did he hide it?"

Andrew scowled with a grim set to his lips. "We don't know."

Jackson drummed his fingernail on the table. "Weren't Ma and him arguing about money that last night?"

Andrew shook his head. "I thought it was over the sow rooting down his damn whiskey mash."

Sophie sighed. "Well, that gives us a little mystery to figure out, doesn't it?"

Andrew, chewing on a crisp piece of pork—it sure didn't need any more salt—couldn't help but agree. Then, still trying to pull the notion of Pa's money out of the air, he sipped on the rich coffee. His mouth flooded with saliva. They'd been missing many good things—and coffee sure was one of them.

She looked hard at them. "You know there were big rumors about just why your pa moved to Texas?"

Jackson blinked at her. "We never heard 'em."

"Course you won't have. But folks said he robbed a rich man on a highway one night and killed him. Took all his money."

"He always said he left Arkansas cause he wasn't going to choose sides between North or South."

"When did he ever worry about what folks thought about him?" Sophie looked pained. "Think about it."

Jackson picked at his food with his fork. "We sure left up there in a gawdawful hurry."

"Pa was always in a hurry." While that was true, Andrew remembered how determined Pa had been that they'd had to move every day, no matter what. "Bad weather never stopped us."

Sophie sipped her coffee. "I figure they had no real evidence or reliable witnesses to say he did it."

Andrew nodded. He recalled waking up in the sleeping loft one night a long time ago in Arkansas and hearing his mother saying, "They'll hang you for sure when they find out."

"No," he'd said. "We're going to Texas."

Next day, they'd left for the Lone Star, raining cat and dogs, roads sloppy, sleet falling. Ma drove the horses. Pa drove the mules. Two wagons—Pa threw half of their things away over her protests so they could get through the endless sea of mud.

Andrew's back ached thinking about the hard work that trip required of him and Jackson. Pa sold his coonhound and two coops of Ma's prized chickens in Fayetteville. Told them all they would only slow them up.

Then Pa'd sold the jersey cow in Alma. Andrew never missed that heifer for a minute. She wouldn't drive and keep up. Pa kept saying to Ma, "Don't worry. I've got the money. I'll buy you more when we get down there."

Jackson interrupted his thoughts.

"Did Pa ever sell that place we had in Arkansas?"

Andrew shrugged. "I thought he sold it and came home with the money the night before we left, but I ain't even sure about that."

"A deputy marshal out of Van Buren came by our place a couple weeks after you all came through, asked my daddy if Pryor Franks had been by there."

"What did he say?" Jackson leaned forward.

"That we ain't seen him."

The boy frowned. "Why'd he say that?"

"Mountain folks are always tight-lipped to lawmen. Especially so 'bout their kin."

Andrew snorted. "He ever find out we went through there?"

"I'm sure he did. Two wagons moving through in bad spring weather weren't hard to notice."

"I never forgot it." Andrew shook his head, staring at the far wall. "It was so maddening, so crazy to fight those muddy crossings and roads with no bottom. He sure might have been running from something bad."

"My life starts in Texas." Jackson leaned back in his chair. "I try not to think about those days before that."

"Maybe he spent all of it." She put her palms on the table to get up. "Or maybe some of it's still around here."

"Maybe." Andrew picked up his plate and fork. "But either way, we don't have it. That means we need to get back to work, go catch more cattle."

She smiled. "Fine idea. I'll have breakfast ready at first light."

In the morning, they were up, saddling, loading, and getting ready before the sun peered over the hill country to the east. Land of the German farmers over that way, centered around New Braunfels. Their pa had liked it there, but had decided to push on west. Said them krauts were too stiff to live around and Lutherans were really just Catholics in disguise.

Andrew moved around the yard in the cool air, checking on what they needed and being sure they had it all. Jackson packed the panniers with what Sophie set out for them to take. Breakfast was coffee, biscuits, fried pork, and some beans she'd put on to cook overnight. The big meal would tide them over till supper, and in a short while they had the door barred, the note up, and were headed again for Swain Creek.

Just past noontime, they chose a campsite on the intermittent stream. Andrew planned to move their camp every third day and be on guard for any unpleasantness. Under the canvas shade Jackson had strung up tree to tree for her, Sophie handed out fried apple pies.

She grinned. "Figured you'd need it."

"We will." Andrew took a bite. God, how he'd missed real food. "Keep that scatter gun handy, though."

"See you at dark."

The job ahead was a tough one. One of them would have to rope one of the steers' heels, take the other yoke off the one not roped, then the one stretched out was set free.

Jackson caught the first one's hind heels easy. He backed up his horse until the left steer was on the ground. Andrew ran in and took off the willow neck-stall and the loose critter didn't take long to get up. By then Andrew had the number two loose and sat on his head while Jackson flipped off his heel catch.

The steers acted much less like deer and were mated for life. By evening he and Jackson only lacked finding two spans of them. Gathering their yokes, they rode back to camp jubilant at their success. Twenty head of yearlings were healing and a lot more gentle. Wearing the three-way mark of the turkey claws on the left side and an underbit on the right ear, they'd know them anywhere. And if there was one thing Texas enforced more ruthlessly than any other, it was brand law.

"Welcome back." Sophie greeted them wearing a white apron they'd never seen on her before. "You boys hear me shoot?"

Jackson stepped down into the dust. "You have some trouble?"

"No, a tom turkey came by to visit me today, and, by God, I invited him to supper."

"Good for him." Andrew laughed, stripping out his latigos.

"Wasn't too good for him."

That evening they feasted on turkey until they were so full Andrew figured he'd bust. Sipping good coffee and sitting cross-legged on the ground, he couldn't believe their new life. Somehow he didn't think it could last. The old man would come back from the dead or something and make their life miserable. He wouldn't even talk about their good fortune out loud with the other two for fear it might break the spell.

He looked up from his cup. Sophie reached out and poked a finger through a hole in Jackson's sorry-looking britches.

"You know, you boys need some real clothing."

Completely unconcerned, Jackson scratched his belly and burped. "Aw, we could patch 'em with deer hide. They're still good enough to do that."

"No, they ain't. And you need a Sunday pair."

Andrew grinned. "Why, we ain't had two pairs of pants in our whole life."

She shook her head impatiently. This was something she obviously wasn't going to let go of. "This ain't Pryor Franks talking. You need to live your life while we're doing all this ranch building."

"What's new pants got to do with living our life?" Jackson asked.

"When you boys become big ranchers, you'll have to be businessmen. Businessmen don't go around with half their butt hanging out of their pants."

Both boys erupted in laughter.

"Us, businessmen?"

"Jackson, you mind my words. You both'll be big men someday. The pride of Texas." She tossed some sticks on the fire and they blazed up. "This cow-catching is all right, but they ain't worth much. You boys ever catch wild horses?"

"Yeah, that's where them horses of ours came from. Pa had a horse he bought off a Mexican and we had burros to ride the first few years. Then we went to trapping mustangs. But horses ain't worth much around here."

"In Fort Worth a riding horse will bring twelve to fifteen dollars. A team will bring forty."

"You saying we need to catch and break horses?" Jackson asked, leaning back on his hand placed on the ground behind him.

The rosy color of the fire reflected off her face. Her words came clear from her lips that looked glossy in the light. "Boys, you can make real money doing that."

Jackson couldn't argue with that. Surprisingly, that was

happening more and more these days. "And we need money, if we're ever going to buy them two pair of pants."

"That's right, brother."

She leaned forward, her sharp eyes looking from one to the other of them. "A man gives you a twenty-dollar gold piece for a twelve-dollar horse. How much change do you give him back?"

"Andrew?"

"Hold on, I'm counting." He used his fingers for the answer.

"Eight dollars." Sophie clacked her tongue at them. "My, my, we need to do arithmetic. You'll get skinned alive in Fort Worth selling horses if you can't count money."

Andrew bobbed his head. "You're right. It's eight."

"Of course, I'm right. But you have to be right, too. Ain't a man living going dicker with a woman about buying a horse."

"How much we got to learn?" Jackson looked pained.

"Plenty. What's two times two?"

"That's easy, it's four."

"Then do the rest."

"I ain't sure I can do them all."

She rubbed her palms on the top of her legs, leaned forward, and began. "Two times three?"

By bedtime they were up to the multiplication table of six. Andrew lay in his blanket and listened to a coyote yip. Six times seven was forty-two. Sounded odd, but she was right no matter about the forty-two, they needed to know numbers to trade horses. Sophie was no dummy, and she might be *all* right before this was all over.

EIGHT

A WEEK LATER, around mid-morning, they'd just turned loose the most recent yoked pair of steers when they had unexpected visitors.

Four men rode toward them from the east. Each rode astride a giant draft horse, and each balanced a musket or shotgun across his leg.

Andrew could see their beards as they got closer. He jerked his head toward them as Jackson recoiled his riata. "German farmers from Mason."

"What're they doing clear out here?"

"We better ride over and see." Andrew swung up on his horse. Out of habit, he adjusted the Colt on his hip.

"And hope they ain't lookin' for trouble," Jackson muttered.

"Good morning." Andrew reined up before them and touched his hat. "You fellows hunting?"

The man with the most gray in his unkempt beard spoke up. "Vee hunting for lost girl. Her name is Margaret. She vas herding sheep and has disappeared. Vee think Indians may take her."

"We ain't seen any Injuns lately. And we ain't seen any girl, either, have we Jackson?"

His brother set his horse and shook his head. "How old is she?"

"Twelve. She has blonde hair, blue eyes."

The man's description turned Andrew's stomach into a rock. She was already some buck's slave. Them Injuns really treated their woman slaves bad, too. Him, Jackson, and Pa had laid down real quiet on a ridge once to watch when a whole party of Comanche went by them. Horses pulling travois and plenty of ponies in their herd made lots of dust. All the Comanche women rode horses, but they had seen some near-naked Mexican women walking behind—slaves whom the braves had whipped on their bare backs to make them keep up.

A picture of the little white girl being driven like that made a sour taste in his mouth.

"Vee better go look for her."

Andrew nodded. "We ain't seen no tracks of any ponies."

The men blinked at each other. One of them pointed to the ground. "There are tracks all over here."

"Those ain't Comanche tracks. Most of these are Jackson's and my tracks from chasing wild cattle. The rest are wild horses."

"Hmm." The man scratched at the side of his face. The group parlayed in German for a few moments, and at last, he turned back to the boys. "Vee will ride vest and try to find her."

Wasn't any damn sense in that, they'd not find nothing. He wanted to shout how stupid they were, but it wouldn't do a damn bit of good.

In defeat, he slumped in the saddle and nodded his okay.

They rode on.

"Damn dumb farmers," Jackson mumbled when they were gone far enough away not to hear him.

"I thought the same thing. Let's call it a day."

"Yeah." Jackson stood in the stirrup and looked around. "I think we've caught most of the wild cattle in this country."

"Eighty-some head of steers wearing our brand." Andrew

wondered how Sophie was doing back in camp. Usually she rode out with them, at least for a while. But the past two days she'd been acting funny and even a little cross, and had stayed close in to camp.

He hoped this fussy business didn't turn into some kind of permanent thing with her.

"How many cattle we got to have to be big ranchers?" Jackson asked as they trotted their horses for camp.

"Maybe a thousand head in Texas."

His brother whistled. "Lordy. Why, we'll be a hundred years getting that many."

He shrugged. It wouldn't be that long at all. "We're pushing on two hundred head now, counting our cows."

"Yeah and some of them got calves this spring." Jackson grinned big. "Good thing we're learning big numbers, ain't it?"

Andrew nodded and they rode over the last high point and headed for the cottonwood line along the thin silver stream. All looked well in camp. He could see campfire smoke when they came over the rise.

The boys dismounted and began to pull their latigos loose on their girths to unsaddle the horses. Sophie was sitting on the ground looking peaked. Andrew finished with his, dropped his saddle, and went over to her.

"You ailing?"

She looked up with a forced a smile and shook her head. "I'm afraid it's just the curse of Eve."

"Huh?" Jackson scratched his head. "What's wrong?"

"Well, you boys are old enough to know that every three weeks women have this spell. They bleed and they don't feel good. It ain't dangerous." She shrugged and dropped her chin. "It just ain't never convenient."

"What'll make it go away?"

"If I was pregnant."

Nothing he could do about that. Andrew went off to hobble his horse. Ma had had that same thing. He remembered her having spells about that far apart when she had no time for them and nothing ever went right for her. Or suited her.

"Least we got someone to blame for her feeling bad." Jackson knelt down and hobbled his pony for the night.

"Who's that?"

"Eve that put the dad-gone curse on her."

"Lord have mercy, Jackson. Why, she's been dead for years and years."

"Huh?"

"That's Adam and Eve from the Garden of Eden in the Bible she's talking about."

"I'll be hornswoggled. That was a real long time ago."

Andrew slapped his pony on the butt and shook his head. "We better go check on the ranch in the morning. These ponies need a rest."

"We'll have to have more horses for this business ourselves."

"Right. Horses to ride and horses for sale. You remember Fort Worth?"

"I think we were there—what, for a day or so?"

"Not any longer than that. We were twelve years old then?"

"About that. You scared of a big place like that? I mean taking horses in there for sale?"

Andrew shook his head. "Naw, not really."

"Good, cause I'll back you all the way."

"What're you two doing now that I don't know about?" Sophie dipped brown beans for them out of the iron kettle.

"How we're going to take horses to Fort Worth." Jackson took a bowl and thanked her.

"Am I going?"

"Lordy, Sophie you're part of us. 'Course you're going."

Andrew clapped her on the shoulder and gave her a hug.

He'd never done that to anyone before, but it felt like the thing for him to do.

She turned, looked at his arm, and nodded in approval. "Good. Then I won't have to stay at home by myself."

"Naw." Jackson hadn't noticed a thing going on between the two of them. His attention was centered totally on his bowl of *frijoles* and how he'd consume them.

"We're going to head home tomorrow. Rest the horses. Get equipped to go mustanging." Andrew picked up his own bowl and stirred the beans in it. "Besides, the yoke man should be here in the next couple of days, too."

She sniffed. "Take a bath?"

"You go right ahead, we won't look." Jackson's voice was muffled around a mouthful of beans.

"I mean *you*, boy. *Both* of you. I've taken two or three baths since we've been out here."

Jackson blinked. "Why we just had one—when was it?"

Seated on the ground with his supper, Andrew shook his head at his brother's question. "Been a long spell. We'll take one here in a few minutes."

His brother groaned. "Are baths going to be a part of that whole businessman thing?"

"Aw, hell." Sophie swore. "It's a wonder you can even catch your horse from upwind."

Jackson laughed. "He has been acting buggery lately."

"That's why." She poured each of them a cup of coffee and then sat down to eat her food.

Andrew told her about the German farmers they'd met earlier and she sounded sad talking about the poor girl's fate. He and Jackson agreed it was a bad business.

After supper, they took a bath and rinsed out their clothes. Andrew noticed the seat of his pants was about worn through. Besides, they fit too tight and made him uncomfortable in the crotch. Where the hell would they ever find a dollar apiece for new ones, though?

Later, he lay in his blanket and wondered more about the notion of Pryor Franks's source of funds. How had he found the money for them to live even as frugal as they did? If so, where was the rest of the money? Maybe it was all gone and that's why Ma and Pa had been arguing that night.

He rolled over on his back and stared at the thousand stars in the sky.

Damn you Pryor Franks, where's it hid at?

NINE

THEY CAME INTO the ranch late in the afternoon, tired and thirsty. Jackson stopped at the well, opened the cover, and dipped buckets of water out to pour in the trough for the horses. The wind must have been down a while—the trough was empty—but the windmill looked okay.

Andrew and Sophie both drank a couple of gourds full of water, then unsaddled and unloaded supplies, and turned the horses out to roam. They left one in the corral, and Andrew scrounged up enough corn for him to eat.

Sophie made supper. After a meal of fried pork and biscuits, Andrew stood in the doorway with his coffee cup and studied the twilight settling down on the pens and rough outbuildings. It felt good to be back home.

But something wasn't right tonight. Amidst the sounds of the birds and insects, he heard something—some*one*—calling for help.

He looked over his shoulder into the kitchen. "You hear that?"

Jackson turned an ear to listen. "Might be a bobcat."

Andrew snatched his gun belt off the peg and strapped it on. "I'll go see."

"Damn it, it could be Injuns, too, Andrew." Sophie stood

and picked up the shotgun from its place in the corner. "It could be a trap. Be careful!"

Andrew ran to the edge of the cleared ground and listened again. When he heard nothing, he cupped his hands around his mouth. "Where are you?"

No answer.

Could someone be in the dry wash over where they'd found the sow the night Ma and Pa had died?

"Help me!"

"I'm coming." He rushed through the grass and brush until he about fell over someone. Stopped in the starlight, he blinked at the sight of a filthy-dirty, naked girl on the ground, her skin so blistered she didn't even look real. She held a hand up like she feared he would hit her.

"You're safe." He scooped her up and ran for the house.

He met Jackson halfway there.

"Who's she? What happened? Where the hell's her clothes?"

Andrew shook his head and kept running. "I don't have any idea. Sophie will know what to do."

"Is it her? The little girl the farmers were looking for?"

"Damnit Jackson, I don't *know*."

Sophie stood in the door of the house, waiting. She gasped when she saw what Andrew carried.

"In here. In here." She waved them into the house, then into the larger bedroom. She pulled the covers back on the iron bed that had belonged to the boys' parents. Then she started issuing orders. "Jackson, go get two buckets of water out of the well. Andrew, you go and start the stove to heat it for me."

"Anything else?"

"Not right now. I can handle it. Now *go*!" She turned to the girl. "Darling, you're safe now."

Andrew stumbled backwards across the small room. Still stunned by his discovery, he tried to clear his thinking. There was no telling how far the little girl had come. How had she ever gotten away from those savages? And where were her clothes?

"Here's the water." Jackson none-too-gently handed him a bucket, sloshing its contents all down Andrew's front in the process.

"Damn it, Jackson. Watch it!"

"Sorry." The blonde boy poked his head back in the bedroom. "Sophie, is she gonna make it?"

Sophie sighed. "I think so. Now you boys get that water heating, then leave us alone in here."

"Yes, ma'am." Jackson backed out of the room and gave her a salute. "We'll be right outside if you need us."

Seated on the ground outside the open door, the boys listened to the little girl's moans and Sophie's apologies. Eventually, Sophie managed to draw out the girl's name—Margaret. Margaret what? Studebaker? Swartz? Hienrich? But the girl would say no more.

After a while, Sophie came out and sat down on the ground beside them. She swept the hair back from her face and breathed a sigh. "She's cleaner. Not clean, but clean*er*. I gave her some laudanum so she could sleep. God only knows when she slept last."

Jackson stirred. "What should we do?"

"Go get some sleep. But don't come in the house in the morning until I get the poor thing dressed."

Andrew had a thought. "Ma's Sunday dress might fit her."

"That would be all right with you two?" She searched their faces for the answer.

Jackson threw his hands up like he'd surrendered. "Ma sure won't need it."

"Fine, I'll use it."

"We'll see you in the morning, Sophie." Andrew got up, ready to go find his blanket. "Holler if you need us."

"Sleep well, boys. You did a good thing tonight."

The boys headed out to the shed. Jackson stuffed his hands in his pockets and looked up at the sky. "Cloud. It may rain."

"Not likely."

"Hey, it rains sometimes in this country."

"I know, but it's dry here compared to Arkansas. Rains up there all the time. Man, I remember getting out of there."

"Rained every day, didn't it?"

"Till we got to Fort Worth, I think."

With their blankets unrolled on the ground behind the shack they called their barn, Andrew yawned and rolled over. "We could use a rain."

"We damn sure could." Jackson put his hands behind his head and stretched. "Hey, Andrew?"

"Yeah?"

"You planning on taking that little girl back?"

"I ain't planning on nothing but sleeping right now."

"Yeah, but you do all the planning."

He sighed. "Night, Jackson."

"Night Andrew. I wonder how in hell she escaped from them red devils?"

Andrew never answered him. He wanted to sleep and escape it all. He recalled carrying the little girl in his arms. She didn't weigh anything. She was so filthy and sun-blistered all over.

How did she ever find their place…?

The bass roar of distant thunder rolling across the land in the night woke him some time later. Groaning, he rolled over and shook Jackson awake. They grabbed their blankets and ran for the shed. From the front door, Andrew saw a light at the house.

Sophie must be up.

He took his canvas poncho off a wall peg and shrugged it on. The rain cover had leather ties at the side and would help keep a person mostly dry working out in a storm. The best feature was as a hail repellant. Many times the poncho had saved him from being beaten to death during a bad storm. Sophie saw him approach the door and waved him inside.

She had cans set around on the floor under several of the worst holes in the roof. The rhythm of the falling drops was almost hypnotic.

He poured himself a cup of coffee and motioned toward the bedroom. "How is she?"

Sophie shook her head. Chewing on her lower lip, she looked ready to cry. "Slept some. Making some sense now. But she may never be normal again."

She shuddered and her knees buckled.

Putting his cup down on the table, Andrew caught her from falling just in time and held her in his arms while she sobbed. "Shh. It's going to be okay."

"She won't ever have a normal childhood, Andrew. They've taken it. They've taken her innocence away from her."

"But she's alive. Isn't that a lot?"

"Living and having a life are two separate things." She backed out and blew her nose in a rag from her pocket. "I'm sorry. I didn't mean to break down."

He brushed her hair out of her face and looked into her eyes. "Sophie, we're family. That's what families are for. We're here for each other. We've only got the three of us."

Her lashes wet with tears, she nodded, seemingly unable to look away. "And one bad lost little lady. I hope she comes out of it."

"And we'll help her all we can, okay?"

Another nod. "Okay."

Jackson appeared in the doorway, his own slicker wet with rain. He peeked in the direction of the bedroom. "She better?"

Sophie sniffled and pulled away from Andrew. "Some."

"Good." He looked at Andrew. "What do we do next?"

"Eat breakfast and then split some firewood."

"I can do that, older brother."

Now standing, Sophie smiled. "How much older?"

"Ma said fifteen minutes."

"She never had any more children?"

Andrew shook his head. "They all died. Some in Arkansas, some here."

"I'm sorry I even asked."

"No. We're family. We ain't got any secrets."

"All any of us got any more is each other." Jackson looked at the floor and scuffed his boot on a pebble.

She brushed her hair back from her face again and wiped her nose. "Nine times nine?"

Jackson looked up and grinned smugly. "Eighty-one."

Later that morning as he and Jackson came in with their arms full of split stove wood, Andrew spotted their guest sitting up in a dress that practically swallowed her up. She rocked some in the small rocker, the one Ma somehow managed to keep through Pa's fits of discarding things on the way down from Arkansas. It had been her granny's small maple rocker.

One look at her peeling face made him want to vomit. He put down the wood and brushed himself off. "She talking?"

Sophie looked as somber-faced as he could recall. "No."

"Guess she will when she gets ready."

"I hope so."

He was busy piling the wood against the wall when the sound of approaching horses came to him.

"Someone's riding up." He rose and he reached for his six-gun. With his fist closed around the smooth redwood grips, he pointed at Jackson. "Go easy, brother. You hear me?"

"I'm always easy. It's them other people that's the problem."

With a grunt, Andrew pushed past him to step outside.

McCory sat his horse in the dooryard, looking wet and angry. This time, though, he'd only brought one of his Mexican gunnies. The sky beyond him boiled with storm clouds, and thunder still rumbled in the distance.

"I see you dumbass boys ain't learned a gawdamn nothing

since the last time I seen you. Well, when I get through with you——" McCory started to dismount his horse when Sophie appeared in the doorway behind the boys and busted off a barrel full of buckshot over his head.

At the shot's report, his blue roan lunged sideways. McCory fell on the ground with his toe hung in the stirrup. The roan's quick movements jerked him down on his back, and had the roan not collided next with the *pistolero's* horse beside him, McCory would have been dragged to his death. But the wreck gave him some slack to kick his boot free, and he scrambled backward from the upset horse like a scorpion on the run.

Jackson pulled his .44 and took a shot at the Mexican, who was trying to draw his own pistol in the sudden confusion. The bullet knocked the *pistolero's sombrero* off and back onto his shoulders and he screamed. Bucking and kicking, the horse took off like a shot, and was soon lost from sight.

Colt cocked and ready, Andrew walked slowly over to where McCory sat on his ass in the mud. With his hat gone and his bald pate shining, he didn't look nearly as tough as he liked to make people think he was. The older man looked up at him with nothing but contempt. "You stupid sumbitch, you could have killed me."

"Who said we were through with you?" Andrew fired a round in the dirt between McCory's legs. "And you better watch who you call a sumbitch."

Bug-eyed in shock, McCory held his hands over his ears. "You could have shot me!"

"I told you I wasn't through with you." He poked his smoking gun barrel in the man's face and cocked the hammer. "Dig out your money. Now, and be quick about it."

"You robbing me?"

"I ain't robbing nobody. I'm taking back what you owe me from the last time we met. Get it out. *Now.*"

Wary-eyed, McCory leaned back and started digging a roll of bills out of his pocket.

Andrew stopped him. "No, I want silver or gold. That Confederate shit ain't worth the paper they print it on."

Struggling with a leather pouch attached to his belt, McCory frowned in Sophie's direction. "Who's she?"

"None of your damned business, is it?" Andrew leaned down and snatched the pouch away. "I'll take that."

"You boys rob me I'm going straight to the Judge. You'll rue this day."

"There ain't no detour on the road to hell gonna let you do that." Jackson held his gun on McCory while Andrew untied the strings on the pouch and opened it.

"Sophie, put up that gun to come hold our money." She walked over and held out her apron. Andrew started picking out gold dollars. "Let's see. There's the seven dollars you took when you and your men attacked us that morning on the creek. I'd say we should add two more to that for the beating you put on us, don't you, Jackson?"

"At least that much, I say."

"And let's see... there's the matter of that three-year-old bay gelding we never found after you set our horses loose. He was a good one, too. You said a good horse brought thirty bucks in Fort Worth, Sophie?"

She nodded.

McCory scowled. "Fort Worth—"

Jackson cut him off by cocking his own hammer. "Shut up."

"Latigos and cinches, five dollars. Two days' lost—twenty dollars." Coin after coin clinked on top of the others in the snowy white of Sophie's apron. "That should just about do it."

Before he could toss the pouch back, though, Sophie stayed his arm. "Don't forget two new Colts and a shotgun. They cost thirty-five dollars."

"Nice. I about forgot them." He tossed in that money, too.

"And the food they pissed on," Jackson reminded him.

"Ten bucks for that." Andrew added it to their treasury. Sophie and Jackson nodded in approval at his unasked question—did they have all McCory owed them now?

Andrew stepped over and jerked the pistol out of McCory's holster. Jamming it in his own waistband, he hauled the man to his feet by the collar. "You ever come back here again, you'll go home feet first. We'll shoot to kill." He shoved him up hard against his horse and reached past him to jerk the Spencer out of the scabbard. "Am I clear?"

"You fu—"

Andrew slammed the butt of the Spencer into his kidneys and McCory went to his knees.

He leaned down and screamed in the man's face. "I asked if I was *clear?*"

"Yeah, yeah." McCory crawled back to his feet, holding his side in obvious pain.

Andrew tossed him the pouch. "Here's your money—what's left of it. Now get your ass out of here and don't ever come back."

"You ain't—heard the last—of this."

"We damn sure better have." Andrew reached in and shook him by the arm. Then, filled with disgust, he turned to Jackson. "Put him on his horse before I kill him."

Grabbing him by his shirt collar and the seat of his britches, Jackson heaved him up over the saddle. McCory managed to get into the seat and gather the reins. All bent over the horn, he went to beating the pony with the reins to make him leave.

Without warning, Jackson turned and ran to the doorway, where he snatched up the shotgun and threw it to his shoulder. "Here's some lead in your ass, mister."

Black powder smoke belched out of the left barrel. Struck by some of the pellets from seventy-five yards, the roan ducked his head and went to bucking, then tore off through the waist-high bunch grass like his butt was on fire.

"Damn it, Jackson, you could have killed him!" Sophie was not happy, and wore a frown to prove it.

Jackson spat in the dirt. "I aimed to."

"No, you were not." Andrew rolled his eyes at his brother's all-to-familiar tough guy routine. "Pa shot at them dang mules we had a dozen times from that far way when they got out. It only stung them."

The younger boy dropped the shotgun to his side and looked away, embarrassed. Then he tried to change the subject. "How much money did we collect?"

Andrew searched the horizon for a long moment, letting Jackson squirm. Then he jerked his head back toward the house. "Let's go inside. We can count it on the table."

Stacked on the table, the money made a small fortune—one hundred and fifty-seven dollar. More than the boys had ever seen in their lives. It was payment for the scars on their faces and those days in desperation when they'd been waiting for Sophie to arrive.

After a while of excited talk and planning, Andrew rapped his knuckles on the table. "Okay, it's settled, then. Tomorrow we go to Mason. We'll buy a load of corn and any other supplies we'll need for gathering horses."

The rain slacked off through the rest of the day. Andrew had never realized just how sorry the canvas roof on the shack was until now. They sure didn't have much worth anything right now, but after today, he decided, that would damn sure change. He remembered what Sophie had said about their future a few days before—that they'd be big-time ranchers someday. After the incident with McCory earlier that day, he damn sure believed it now. Come hell or high water, he'd make it happen.

The next morning, they were up early readying for their ride into Mason. Jackson took charge and picked the gentlest horse in their corral for the little girl to ride, a buckskin mare they called Pumpkin. After breakfast, they lifted her to Pumpkin's back. Then they mounted their own horses and set out at a jog. It was cool and cloudy, but the sun and humidity would soon be up and boiling.

Andrew noted how well she rode. He'd worried about her riding with only a pad, but she knew how to ride. They made a few stops to water the horses and empty their own bladders, but still managed to arrive in Mason by early afternoon.

The gossip started as soon as they entered town, and before long, many women came running, their skirts high, shouting, "They've found her! They've found her! They've brought her back alive." Workingmen joined the women and soon encircled the riders as they approached the courthouse stairs.

Andrew, Jackson, and Sophie dismounted and moved toward Pumpkin and her precious cargo. As they pulled Margaret down off the mare, a tall bearded man emerged from the crowd.

"Thank God you've found her. God bless all of you!"

The boys looked at each other, unsure of what to do. Sophie picked the little girl up and cradled her against her breast. "We're happy to have helped. Is her family here?"

Beside the bearded man, a young woman stepped forward. "I'm her aunt."

"Is her mother here, too?"

"We will send for her. They live on a farm west of here."

Andrew and Jackson shared another glance. They'd probably passed it on their way in.

Sophie hesitated. She wanted to tell the aunt what had happened to the little girl, but didn't want to say it out loud. Finally, she leaned over and whispered in her ear.

The woman straightened. "I can care for her at my house until her mother can come."

"Wait!" The big man with the beard held up his hands. "This woman and these two men are heroes. They have returned a child to us and taken great care of her. Let us feed them lunch and see what we can do for them."

A cheer went up from the crowd. Two serious-looking men stepped forward and took the reins of their mounts. They were the town's liverymen, they would see to the horses' care while they were occupied. Then Andrew, Jackson, and Sophie were herded to a nearby café where more people crowded around them.

The tall man was the town sheriff. "My name is Herman Stone. Will you introduce yourselves?"

"Um... Andrew can do that." Jackson looked embarrassed. He looked at the snowy-white napkin on the table like he'd never seen one before.

Sophie leaned over to in his ear. "It's a napkin. You put it in your lap so it doesn't soil your britches."

At the head of the table, Andrew stood and removed his hat. "My name is Andrew Franks. This is my twin brother, Jackson. And this lady with us is our cousin and guardian, Sophie Grenada. We own the Turkey Track Ranch thirty miles or so west of here." He picked up a glass and took a drink of water. "A while back, some of your men came through our land looking for Margaret. We hadn't seen her, nor saw any Comanche working the area. But when we returned to our homestead a few days later, we heard a voice crying in the night. We went out to look, and that's when we found here. We brought her to the house. Sophie has cared and nursed her ever since, until we thought she was strong enough to make the trip back."

The applause began and the sheriff asked them all to stand. Andrew couldn't decide who was more embarrassed of the three of them.

Finally, they were allowed to sit again, and some cute teenage girls began moving around the tables, serving heaping plates of food. Jackson's gaze came up from the table and whirled around, finally locking on to one, in particular, a lithe red-headed girl with a freckles and sparkling green eyes.

Andrew hid a smile as his eyes met Sophie's.

The sheriff laid a hand on Andrew's shoulder. "What else can we do to thank you for what you've done?"

"Ah, well..." Andrew scratched his head. "We'd hoped to buy a wagonload of corn while we were in town today."

"You're money's no good here. We'll fill a wagon and bring it to your ranch. In gratitude for what you've done for us."

"I have the money to buy it."

"No, all the farmers will contribute and bring you a load of corn for what you did here today."

"That's damn generous of them."

"We're just thankful that we could help Margaret." Sophie wiped her mouth on her napkin.

Beside her, Jackson's eyes lit up. "So *that's* what this gawdamn thing is for, huh?"

Andrew and the sheriff both erupted in laughter, followed by Sophie. Jackson's face turned red, especially as the girl who had captured his attention happened to be walking by.

"What? I've never seen one before!"

"Anything else we can do?" the lawman asked.

"I know you're not the law out around our ranch, but we've had a problem with a man, one of our neighbors." He went on to explain about their little war with McCory and what all had happened. "I imagine he's gone to the judge by now and sworn out a warrant after our argument—what with the way we collected the money he owed us."

"I can get that set aside."

"We aren't crooks, sir. But by damn he's been miserable to live around."

"Don't worry. I'll tell Judge Watkins the facts and he'll listen."

"We really appreciate it." Andrew shook his hand. "If you only knew what a load that is off my mind."

"I heard that." Jackson used the napkin to wipe his chin, more than a little self-consciously. "Save us another fight."

"And since you big ranchers don't have to pay for any corn," Sophie put in slyly, "we're going to march on over to the mercantile and buy both of you two pair of overalls."

Andrew laughed. "And a new dress for you Sophie."

"Aw, I don't need one."

"If we're going to wear new clothes, so are you."

Jackson, his mouth full, nodded his agreement. Then he wiped his mouth with the napkin again. "Boy, they sure set a good table."

The sheriff shook his head. "You ain't seen nothing' yet. Dessert's next."

Andrew wasn't too sure he could hold anymore, but he did. Blackberry cobbler and real whipped cream. It was as if they'd known his weaknesses all along.

Later, they learned that the little girl's name was Margaret Bauer. Her mother and father arrived later in the evening at the street dance the town had thrown together for their visiting guests of honor and thanked them. The parents were so grateful, they broke down in tears, hugging them over and over again.

Accordion music came wafting down the street, and Sophie stood and danced with several men. Jackson took lessons from some girls his age, but wasn't skilled at it. It didn't matter, though, he enjoyed their attention—especially that of the little redhead that seemed to haunt his steps.

Andrew spoke to a few of the local farmers. They'd also heard that horses brought a good price in Fort Worth. Many had been used up in the ongoing war. But one man brought up something Andrew had never heard before. If he and Jackson ventured up north, there was a better-then-even chance they'd be drafted for service in the Confederate Army.

The town elected to put them up for the night in the local hotel. Before they turned in, Andrew pulled Sophie off to the side to talk. "Some of the farmers I've been talking to say Confederate draft men would snatch us up if we went up to Fort Worth."

She sighed. "Lordy, yes, I forgot the war is still going on. You two can't appear there. They'd damn sure send you off packing a gun."

"That closes our horse business, then."

"No, we can hire an old man to go up there with me. I can sell them."

They stood looking at each other for a moment. "I'll tell Jackson. I think he wanted to skip going up there, anyway."

"Who wouldn't, with as many girls as he has following him around." She laughed. "This has been a good trip. We've made some friends and we've learned a lot. This is exactly the kind of thing we need to be doing more of in the future."

TEN

THEY RODE HOME the next morning decked out in their new clothing, their horses piled high with supplies and the goods necessary to capture wild horses. Sophie sang songs most of the way. Jackson hummed along with her.

Andrew had bought ammo for the Spencer repeating rifle he'd taken from McCory and spent some time figuring its ins and outs. The .50-caliber rifle required tubes to feed it. They had bought some of them, too. The gunsmith in Mason had told him it was a very good gun and would be ideal for its firepower. They were set up to use it, if necessary.

The ranch looked pretty much like they'd left it. They made plans to go stake out some mustangs in the morning. That required setting up a trap, and *that* would mean some fence building. They'd bought rolls of slick wire to tie up poles.

Andrew thought hard about where they'd need to set up when they rode up on a water box they'd first set when they'd moved here. Their father had insisted they have set it up almost before they'd unpacked a thing. Andrew never could figure what the old man's hurry had been about making a water trap out of cypress wood and burying in it in the sand creek bed to collect water.

A few days later, they had it built. They tested it that day on their horses and it worked like a charm. By the time they rode home, Sophie had dinner waiting on them. They'd need to wait for the corn delivery to actually trap more horses—they couldn't keep them fed, otherwise. In the meantime, though, Jackson—the better scout—needed to find some good horses to trap. So he rode out by himself for a few days to have a look around.

For his part, Andrew set about catching up on the housekeeping work they'd let fall down since Pa's death. He repaired and saddle-soaped all of their leather goods. That took him almost a whole day. Then, since he still had a good hour before sundown, he decided to climb up and make sure the windmill was good and greased. That didn't take him long, either.

But coming down the ladder from the top, a thought struck him. How in the hell had the old man paid for the damn windmill. It seemed like it cost something like seventy dollars to have built, if he remembered right. There were so many things he had no clue as to how the old man afforded them. There *had* to have been a source, but whatever it had been, he'd kept it a damn tight secret.

Sophie was hanging clothes on the line in the strong South Texas wind when he found her. He told her again of his thoughts, and she shaded her eyes to look up at the windmill's whirling blades. "How *did* he pay for it?"

"Good question. He paid them in silver coins."

Then he had another notion. The two wagons they'd brought from Arkansas were still parked by the house, the boards shriveled up from the weather and several years of non-use. Pa had sold his draft animals to the Germans when they'd first arrived, but said he might need the wagons again one day.

She saw him turn that way. "What?"

"The wagons. I never looked close at them." He walked over toward that side of the house and looked at them closely.

"What are you thinking?"

He didn't move. "If that sumbitch somehow brought a bunch of money along, he would have had to have it somewhere on one of these wagons. On them or in them."

"Well, let's take a look."

So they did. Using a crowbar and a shovel, they began prying loose every board and nail they could find.

Finally, while on his back underneath the wagon closest to the back—the one Pa had driven, Andrew found a box attached to the bed. It was nailed shut and had no hatch.

"Hey, Sophie? Bring me a hammer."

She was on her knees by the wheel. "Find something?'

"Maybe. There's a box here and it has no door on it."

Sophie disappeared for a moment, then came right back, this time with a claw hammer. She handed it to him and backed away.

Andrew spun the hammer in his hand and took a deep breath. This was the moment of truth. Gripping the tool firmly, he raised his arm. Three hard smashes and the old wood splintered like a rotten watermelon.

"*Holy shit!*" A waterfall of silver coins rained down on him and spilled across the ground in a stream. "Pryor Franks, you old sumbitch. You did *have* money all those years. We're *rich!*"

"What? *What?* Oh, my Lord!" Sophie ducked down and snatched up a handful. She held one up to the light. "By God, they're silver dollars."

"Hundreds of them. *Thousands!* Just wait till Jackson hears about this."

"I can't hardly wait." Sophie giggled like a little girl. "I bet this was the money he stole up there."

"No telling, but he left it to us."

"Jackson may have forgotten, but I'll never forget how I pushed and worked on these two wagons night and day to get us here. Worst days of my life. Damn him, anyway."

She shook her head. "They were mine, too."

There was something in her voice again—not much, just a small catch that warned of something more. Right now wasn't the time or the place to ask about it—too much to think about lying on his back while a river's worth of money spilled out on him—but he would soon.

Damn, how much money was in this box? Was there more? How many people had Pa killed for it?

Wordlessly, Sophie got up and went into the house. She came back with her arms filled with kettles. On their hands and knees, they started filling them with silver coins in the fading light.

"Who was it he robbed?"

She shrugged. "I never heard that. They had lots of money, though, if the rumors were right."

"Why didn't I look at this earlier?" He shook his head.

"Who knew where he hid it?"

"I agree. Damn, I feel like a crook myself."

"The people had this probably don't exist anymore, what with the war and all. Things are lost and aren't ever to be found. No one ever came around looking for it after you got here?"

"No."

"Then I don't think anyone knew where you all were at until I got the letter from that judge." She glanced over at him. "Andrew, this still may only be part of it."

"Well, it will sure help us. How much you think is here?"

"Nine hundred or so, I'd wager."

"I bet so. Wait till Jackson gets back. He won't believe we've been walking by it all this time. Hell, I haven't looked over that other one yet, either."

They carried the heavy bowls inside one at a time, putting them on the table. She went to work stacking coins in piles of fifty each. When it had all been counted, there was eight hundred forty dollars total. After talking it over, they decided to store it in a small trunk his mother had used, hidden under one of the beds.

Jackson arrived home a little while after dark and found his brother and their guardian in one hell of a good mood. Sophie fixed him supper while Andrew told him about their discovery.

Jackson was so excited, he knocked his hat off his head to the floor. "Why didn't we even look at that old wagon before now?"

Andrew laughed. "No telling. We can search the other one tomorrow, though. You find any good mustangs?"

"Three bunches of them nearby. I think we can make one trap and catch all of them in it, eventually."

"You did well, brother."

Sophie put a steaming plate down in front of each of them, "Eat, rich ranchers. You need your strength."

Jackson shook his head and reached up to squeeze her arm. "You're good luck for us."

"You're smart. You would have found it sooner or later." She grinned. "Six times six."

"Thirty-six."

She stuck out her tongue at him.

Andrew rubbed his chin. "Whether we would have or not, the important thing now is that we have it. And we'll use it for the benefit of us all."

Sophie sat down at the table with her own plate, her eyes twinkling. "Amen to that."

They found nothing under the second wagon the next day. While disappointing, it did nothing to alter their good moods. They had a plan, and they knew now what they needed to do to make it work. Instead of resting on their laurels, they got organized to go build their mustang-catching pen.

The water source Jackson had found was perfect, hemmed in by bluffs on all sides. All they'd need to do was drive the horses inside, then block the few places where they could escape.

Slashing brush and wiring poles to turn back potential escapees, they worked around the big circle. From her vantage point on the bluffs above, Sophie kept an eye out for any threats with a brass telescope she'd bought in Mason. Andrew wasn't sure they'd really heard the last of their old friend McCory. They'd heard nothing from him or the judge so far. Perhaps the Mason County Sheriff had stopped them like he promised.

Better safe than sorry, though.

Taking a seat in the shade of a cottonwood, Andrew bit into one of the pork sandwiches Sophie had brought along. He'd told her soon after she'd arrived that he'd always liked sourdough bread, so she'd started making special sandwiches with it just for him.

Sophie came and plopped down beside him. With her hat tipped back on her head, she stretched out her long legs and groaned. "I haven't seen anyone all day."

He took another bite. "That's a good thing. We'll have this trap all set in another day or two."

"How hard will it be to get them in here?"

"The horses? Well, they won't dance on in, but we'll damn sure get them in here."

Jackson came around the side of their tree, wiping sweat from his brow. "This is a lot bigger operation than we ever tried before."

She shaded her eyes and looked up at him. "What do you mean? The pen?"

Andrew finished off his sandwich and rubbed his hands on his britches. "We only caught a handful at a time when we tried before. That's what he's worried about."

"What if we get a hundred head in down there?" Jackson looked out over the watering hole. "We'll have to sort out the ones we want. Some of those old stallions will eat you up."

"We'll have to shoot some if they get that mad."

Jackson nodded, looking glum. "I bet we have to."

"It'll work, brother."

"You're more certain than I am."

Two days later they had the pen finished. The plan of

attack was simple. They needed to start trailing the first group
of mustangs they wanted driven into the corral until they came
within range of the large opening. That meant one rider out
wide, swinging a rope to tag them and keep them moving until
they could spook them on into the pen.

Jackson took the first day, and Andrew and Sophie brought
him a fresh horse and lunch at mid-day. He squatted in the shade
of the cottonwoods and talked to them between bites.

"They don't act like they like our trap."

Andrew shrugged. "Keep them moving. They'll break that
way when we start putting pressure on them."

"Not today, anyway."

"We've got lots of time."

"Then you can do this tomorrow."

"No problem."

On the third day, when Jackson had them close to the opening,
Andrew and Sophie rode in from the right and left, shouting
and waving towels over their heads. The mustangs spooked and
thundered for the mouth of the trap just like they'd planned, the
three screaming riders stampeded them inside. The mustangers
slid to a halt to pull the gates hastily into place.

Andrew's heart nearly beat its way out from under his
breastbone as they struggled to get the closure up and finish the
job. The others met him in the middle, where they tied the last two
posts together before all three collapsed in the dust. Winded but
proud, they shared the moment with grins and heavy breathing,
squeezing each other's hands.

They'd completed the first part of their plan.

Now came the hard part.

They needed to fix each of the mustangs they wanted to keep
with a log drag—one hell of a dusty, gritty job that would take both
the boys to get done. One brother would rope one, while the other
ran another rope around the mustang's neck—slack enough not to

choke it—with a log attached to the end so as to drag behind the the animal's heels. That took them three days, and a good number of bumps and bruises, to boot.

Next they had to cut out the un-roped horses, colts, mares, and studs. That required another two days.

By then, though, they were down to right at forty head of weary, fought-out mustangs.

On the last day, they cut out eight of the remaining herd and haltered them. Then, with two mustangs to each side, the boys took them home. The horses learned lots about leading going to the ranch. Their riders did too, but in a day and a half they had them all home.

They'd sent Sophie over to Mason a few days before to buy a couple tons of hay. As they rode into the homeplace that afternoon, she had two wagonloads of hay in the process of being forked off into the corral.

Because of the hard work, they were making progress. A horse doctor from Kerrville had agreed to come out to the ranch and castrate the new arrivals for two dollars apiece and let the boys brand them while they were tied down. Dr. Gardner arrived with four Mexican boys before the week was over to neuter the males that ranged from two to five years old.

Doc looked over the horses in the pen. "This is quite a large project for you two boys, isn't it?"

Jackson started to object to the statement, but Andrew cut him off with a look. He didn't like the implication, either, but the old man's opinion mattered not a whit to him.

He shrugged and kept his tone level. "Have to start somewhere, I guess."

"These horse ain't worth much around here."

"There are places around where they'll bring some cash."

Gardner shook his head. "I hope you do well with them, but I'd say you are wasting your time."

Andrew's teeth ground together at the doctor's patronizing tone. It was time to change the subject before he lost his temper. "I guess we'll start gelding them in the morning?"

"Yes."

Damn that conceited old bastard, anyway. Why did everyone think they were going to fail? He tried to shake it from his mind. Things kept moving along, they were going to make more than enough money to survive on. Those forty horses would help them get there. They might be kids, but they never had a chance to be children. That was what folks like the Doc didn't understand. They had over two hundred cattle in their logbook. They'd have lots more before the year was over. They'd have to show all of them.

Sophie saw the look on his face when they came in for supper. "You two look like your dog just died. What's wrong?"

"Nothing."

"I know you better than that, kid. Spill it."

"I don't understand why people think we're gonna fail just 'cause we're 'just boys.'"

"I don't think you'll fail."

"Yeah, but you're special."

"Why, thank you, young sir." She smiled. "I'm quite fond of you, too. Just remember, you'll be the—"

"I know, I know." He sat heavily in his chair and grinned. "The pride of Texas."

"And Arkansas. Now, *eat*. You'll be busy with all this, I can tell."

In spite of Sophie's peptalk, nothing was resolved for him. Andrew had trouble sleeping that night, then woke early the next morning to supervise the vet and his crew working on the mustangs.

Doc Gardner and his bunch were smooth at what they did. They used a running W on each patient, laying them down with a minimum of stress. He and Jackson did the branding until mid-morning, when Doc told them his men would finish branding them as they worked.

Andrew thanked him and told him he was very qualified to handle the job. Gardner seemed pleased by the compliment.

Things moved on from there. The mustangs learned to be tied and lead. Ten of the tamer ones were saddled and had a hoof tied up to a saddle horn or a rope tied around them. In three days, the boys were riding them.

An older cowboy by the name of Jim Green showed up one day looking for work. The boys talked to him about taking ten of the broke horses to Fort Worth to sell them. Green considered it and agreed to try it. Andrew told him they'd pay him a dollar a day for his expenses, and any horse he sold for over thirty dollars, they would split with him 50/50.

They rode the fire out of the new mounts for the next few days, getting them good and broken in. At the end of the week, Green loaded up a packhorse and headed off to the Fort Worth Stockyards with their first string of horses for sale.

Andrew didn't sit back for a minute. He and Jackson broke more horses to ride. During one of their noon breaks, Jackson joked about being tired. Andrew teased him about having two pair of pants and he was already getting lazy. Ten minutes later, Sophie came out into the dooryard to find Andrew down in the dirt, hogtied, with his younger brother sitting on him.

Jackson just grinned. "He had the guts to call me lazy."

Jim Green was back ten days later, out of horses and loaded down with three hundred dollars in cash.

"I tell you, boys, Fort Worth needs more horses."

"How many?"

"As many as we can turn out." Green pushed back his hat and scratched his head. "I can sell ten more as soon as I get back."

That night, the family held a round table discussion with their new horse trader and decided to send him back into the fire. In another three weeks, he'd managed to sell all their horses and had several orders for more.

The plan was working. They'd earned almost a thousand dollars in just two months of horse wrangling.

They were in business.

A few days later, Palo Pinto, the diminutive Mexican adobe bricklayer they'd loaned their burro to, returned at last to honor his promise. As was typical, Jackson got mouthy about the delay until Sophie had silenced him with a slap across the back of the head.

"Better late than never. Remember that and maybe you'll start to think before you speak, Jackson."

Without missing a beat, Sophie took Palo and the two young helpers he'd brought with him out to a small hillock overlooking the homestead. Here, she told him, was where they wanted their new big house to be built. Palo surveyed the ground and called it good, but cautioned her that he must make hundreds of adobe bricks before starting on construction. At that point, Sophie took him to Andrew.

Always on top of things, Andrew found a nearby source of adobe to dig up and Palo and his assistants started making bricks. Using a wooden form, they made eight bricks at a time, then stacked them to dry in the sun after they shrunk in the mold.

Over supper one night, Jackson asked to hire some *vaqueros* and gather more mustangs for sale. They would need the money, he said. After all, there damn sure wasn't much else making money at the moment. Andrew found his brother's logic sound and encouraged him to try.

A few days later, they threw up a canvas cook shack to feed all the new hands. It was rude—just a framework of wood covered in canvas—but it was more than enough to do the job. Andrew scrounged up a large used sheet-iron stove and hired a Mexican to bring wood to cook with. The cloth sides of the shack could be tied up or down depending on the dust blowing and storms.

With things going so well at the homestead, Andrew decided

one morning to leave Sophie in charge and ride out to check on Jackson's progress with the mustangs. Truth be told, with most of his days now devoted to actually *running* the ranch—decisions, numbers, forecasts—he missed the old days of *working* it.

He found the camp right where he thought he would, out near the water trap near their original campsite from a few months before. It was empty, though, except for a pretty young Mexican woman in an apron.

Reining up, he tipped his hat. "Ma'am. I'm, uh, sorry to bother you, but I'm looking for Jackson and his mustang crew."

"*Sí*, they are going to put the horses in the big pen today. They're all tired of trailing them around. My name is Sabrina. I am their cook." She gestured to a small canvas shade to work under and a tabletop covered with utensils.

"Thanks, Sabrina. Uh... I'm Jackson's brother, Andrew."

"Oh, you are the *patrón*, then."

His face grew hot. "No, I'm simply Andrew."

"If you'd like to see them, *patrón*, I think they're working to the north today." She pointed. "That way."

"Thank you, ma'am." He touched his hat again and galloped off in that direction. He reached a high point and saw the dust boiling up in the distance. They must have the new herd on the move. As embarrassed as he'd been at Sabrina's deference—especially her use of the title *patrón*—her presence in the camp told him that his brother was doing well for himself. He'd let Jackson handle this project by himself, and hiring a camp cook was one of those details not everybody thought about the first time out. Good for him. Success with his first individual project on the ranch would be a good boost for his confidence.

After a few minutes, Andrew decided he'd head west and join the crew for the final drive into the trap. As he spurred his horse and dropped off the ridgeline, he bumped into one of Jackson's *vaqueros*.

He reined up by the man."Hi, there. I am Andrew Franks."

"*Sí!* I am Alex. You are the *patrón.*"

"No, I'm Andrew."

The *vaquero* checked his horse at the sight of the oncoming herd leader emerging out of a cloud of dust. "They are coming. We must turn them here, *señor.*"

"I'm with you."

The lead mare thundered into sight and when she acted like she wouldn't turn, they let off pistol shots in the air to convince her where to go. Then they charged her. She started to cut ahead of them, but riding full steam to her left, they managed to send her south, instead, right into the canyon. The rest would follow her.

In the boiling dust, the mustangs charged into the trap and the shouting *vaqueros* reined up at the entrance. Flooded with adrenaline, they hooped and hollered about their victory, shooting their pistols in the air. They'd done it.

Jackson, his face caked with a muddy mixture of dirt and sweat, reined up beside him, grinning broadly. "Glad you made it, brother."

"Nice chase, Jackson. You've got a big herd this time."

"Come on." Jackson pointed to the entrance. "We have a way to separate them, as well, now we've got them."

With the dust settling some, he could see the series of pens they'd built to work them. Standing in the stirrups he took his time admiring their work. "Nice setup."

"We can use them for cattle, too."

Andrew nodded his understanding. "You've done well. How many hands do you have?"

"Not counting the cook, six *vaqueros.*"

"What do they cost?"

"Fifteen bucks a month and food. You can't find any *gringos* that'll do work for that."

"Not here in Texas. They're all off fighting the war."

"Can we brand some more cattle while I have these boys?"

"Sure. How many do you want?"

"Men or cattle?"

Andrew laughed. "I'm talking cattle."

Jackson shrugged. "Oh, a thousand head should make us competitive."

"We'll have to work on the horse deal, too. It can still make us some money right now."

"You still got your horse trader?"

"Oh, yeah. Jim likes selling horses for us. He's even got some new markets up there north of Fort Worth."

"Three weeks, we'll have him some prospects, then. We won't need the horse doctor. I have some men that can geld them."

Andrew punched his younger brother in the arm. "We may have a ranch someday, boy."

He was proud of Jackson's accomplishment. He'd always been so headstrong—a hard worker, sure, but not a thinker, and always ruled by his temper rather than his brain. This *vaquero* business told Andrew that he had a real partner emerging.

He grinned. "We don't even need Pa to tell us how to do it."

"I think we may well make it without him." Jackson agreed with somber nod. Then he grinned. "Only just barely, though."

They rode back to the camp at the water trap. The *vaqueros* rattled off their names as he shook hands with each of them. At Jackson's urging, he spent the night with them out under the stars. Jackson had big plans to separate the mares, colts, studs, and plugs from the usable horses they intended to start breaking later that day.

"We'll bring the sale horses on over to the ranch where the hay is at."

"Be hard as hell to get hay hauled out here."

"Ain't that the truth. Can Sophie handle feeding some of the men while we break horses?"

"I'm sure she will, but I'll talk to her. You know she wants us to succeed. She's a part of us."

"I know. I just wanted to check." Jackson yawned and stretched his arms out wide. "Well, brother, I need to get up there and start separating."

"You be careful."

"Yeah, well, at least I won't have Pa up there chewing on my ass all damned day."

They parted with a handshake. Andrew loaded up his horse and got home mid-day.

Sophie was hard at work cooking in her new canvas food shack. She dried her hands and came over to talk. "How's Jackson?"

He shrugged. "He's got lots of horses penned. Maybe twice what we had the first time. His guys will be bringing some in over the next few days. We'll need to feed them while they're here."

"How many does he have?"

"Six and a cook."

"Oh, he has a cook?"

"Pretty girl named Sabrina."

"Where'd he get his supplies?"

"I'm not certain. But he has them fed."

She frowned. "I better look at the hay we have and order some more, just in case. We're going to have lots of horses to break and feed. Jim was by here today and wondered when he'd have some more for him to sell."

"I bet in two, three weeks they'll have him some. Jackson's really got things organized out there."

"He got that from you. Anything else?"

"Not a thing. How are the builders?"

She smiled. "They're laying bricks. He's got the plan laid out and they've switched over to making bricks for half the day and laying them the other half."

"How's our money holding?"

She made a face. "I don't know what Jackson's spent, but we'll make him show us."

"That's a good idea."

"I think we're fine. We have over fifteen hundred dollars now."

"Good. It is damn hard to earn it."

"Horses have helped."

"I agree, and we haven't been drafted so far."

Sophie shook her head. "I have nightmares about that."

Andrew gazed off at the heat waves distorting the landscape off in the distance. "Desperate as they are for soldiers I bet they'd get us the first time we rode down the street in Fort Worth."

"Probably."

In two weeks, the *vaqueros* had two dozen mustangs green broke. The horses were still a little stiff from the gelding process, but Jim Green proclaimed them ready for the trip to Fort Worth, anyway. One of the older hands went with him to help handle the horses. When they were gone for over ten days, Andrew began to worry that something had happened to them. Thankfully, they showed back up just two days later.

Over dinner that night, Jim told them why they were later than they'd expected. "Harder to sell them this trip, but I have the next twenty sold for thirty-five apiece. He wanted forty head. He's going to try to drive some cattle up into Missouri. Says they're out of meat up there and thinks he can get through the lines and sell them."

Andrew nodded. "We can deliver him that many horses if he don't mind them being a little less green broke."

"He's a wheeler and dealer. I think either the Yanks or the Rebs will shoot him when he tries to cross their lines."

"That wouldn't be our fault."

Jim smiled and shook his head. "He's got silver money. That Confederate paper is really worthless these days. Hardly anyone will accept it."

"Take him that many. Get the silver and we'll all celebrate. You can take three of the boys with you to deliver them."

Jackson rode in later that evening. Andrew sat him down with Jim and explained the plan.

"Hell, yes, let's do it."

Jim held up a warning finger. "We might not get them sold. But I'll try like hell to find buyers. There ain't no one got any help to round up horses. The boys are all off soldiering. They can't figure out how we can get them, either."

"Keep them guessing." Jackson clapped him on the shoulder. "We still have horses to sell."

By the end of the month, Sophie had over three thousand in silver and gold in their treasury. Business was good.

A man came down from Fort Worth to find them. His name was Euel Dawes, and he'd heard of their operation through Jim Green. He drove a buckboard and wore a suit with a gold watch fob dangling from a silvery vest.

Andrew met him in the dooryard, shook his hand, and offered him a tour.

"I see you've got *vaqueros* hired."

"Yes, sir. They're a great help to us."

"There ain't no cowboys you can hire." Dawes sounded disgusted. "That damn war ain't going good, either. I need some partners. That's why I came on down to see you."

"What for?" Andrew showed him into the house and waved him into a chair. Sophie brought in two mugs of coffee.

"I want to gather a thousand head of cattle, drive them to New Orleans."

"You do that. I don't want no part of them swamps." Andrew had no ambition to go that way—he'd heard all the tales about the route through Southern Louisiana.

"I can get us forty a piece for steers over there."

And the money'd probably be in worthless Confederate scrip,

any way. Andrew shook his head. "No way, mister. We don't need any part of that."

The businessman fixed him with an ugly scowl. "Then what are you going to do? Wait till the damn war is over and take nothing for them?"

"I ain't driving nothing over there. And that's my final word on the matter, sir."

At that point, Dawes gave up on convincing him and stormed off as thought Andrew had insulted his ancestors.

Andrew found Sophie inside the cook shack after Dawes had flung gravel across the yard with his quick departure. She gave him a knowing look. "He have any earthshaking ideas?"

"No. He wants to drive cattle east through all those rivers and swamps to New Orleans. I'm not web-footed enough to go there."

"Where's there a market for beef?"

"It won't be east. The money's all in the north."

"What can you do about it?"

"I may go north and have a look around. There has to be a market somewhere. You, me, and Jackson need to sit down and draw up a plan."

The private talk of the Turkey Track Ranch managers took place late that night around the supper table, after all the hands had gone to bed.

Jackson got right to the point—as usual "What will we do with our cattle?"

"I don't want to drown them in the rivers and swamps between here and New Orleans." Andrew shook his head. "I've talked to drovers who went there. It's all swamps, rivers, and marshes. Damn snakes and huge gators. I'm not going there. I want to ride up to Fort Smith and see if there are any markets around there. That way I could stay in Texas and the Indian Territory to deliver them. Those people in Missouri hate Texas cattle. They're afraid our stock carries Texas tick fever. Those people at Fort Smith are

Southerners. We came from there. It won't be a big drive. That would be the best we can do for now."

"Who's going with you?"

Andrew gave him a funny look. "I planned to go by myself."

His brother didn't like that one bit. "What do you think, Sophie? I think he needs someone to go with him."

She nodded. "That's wild country, Andrew. Listen to your brother. Two'd be better than one to go up there."

"And who would that be?"

Jackson folded his hands on the oilcloth tabletop. He was the picture of calm. "We'll need to find someone."

"Jackson will need to stay here and look after things. You two have more than ten employees. You have to have one boss here."

Andrew cleared his throat. "*We.*"

"Okay." She smiled shyly. "*We* have that many. Surely you have an idea of who could go with you."

"The guy who has the most experience at sales is Jim Green."

She wasn't buying. "He's a little long in the tooth to be a bodyguard, don't you think?"

"But he's sold things. He has ideas I don't. If we can leave now, we may have a market this fall we can reach."

"Skip that." Jackson raised his index finger and shook it at his brother. "We need him here to sell horses and keep that income coming in. I have a young guy named Philippé. He's a good shot and tough enough to protect your backside. I'd rather have him watch out for you."

"Then I guess I better meet him."

"He'll be here tomorrow. You'll see. He's sharp."

"You're going to have to wear boots, though." Sophie nodded toward the floor. "The barefoot cattle baron business is a little crude."

"Dress us up, Sophie." Andrew laughed. "Hell, my feet don't fit shoes."

She shook her head. "There are boots made to fit your foot. I promise you."

"How much do they cost?"

"Listen, Pryor Franks, stop asking about costs. I ain't never seen a barefoot banker or cattle buyer in all my life. You want to be taken seriously? Buy some damn boots."

Jackson chuckled. "His feet are so big, Pa had Ma make him up some Injun boots."

Sophie considered this. "Yeah, they might work. Make a pattern of both your feet. Maybe I can make you a pair you can wear when you do business."

"Two pair of pants and now boots. Hell, we're going to be a couple of dandies, Jackson."

"One more thing," she said, holding her finger up in a motherly fashion. "Before you leave, we're going to Mason. I want to buy you a good hat. A hat sets off a man. You know what I mean?"

Andrew shook his head.

"You stop and think. That sheriff at Mason wore a good hat. See how he stood out?"

He chuckled, reached out and rubbed her shoulder. "We love you, Sophie. Make us big-time ranchers."

"Hell, yes." Jackson slapped the table with his palm. "You ain't hurt us a bit."

Andrew met Philippé the next day. The young man, who was in his early twenties, said he'd very much like to go along on a business trip. So they walked back behind the barn and Andrew asked him if he could shoot.

"Oh, I can use this old pistol."

"Good. Let's bust some bottles. Is it loaded?"

"*Sí.*" He smiled politely.

There were several old bottles in a pile. They'd picked them up in town a while back for him and Jackson to use for target practice.

"I'm going to call you Phil. I want you to bust four or five."

And the man did that.

Andrew's eyebrows rose. "Wow. Good shooting. You must've practiced a lot. Most folks can't hit a barn with one."

"My father say, 'If you choose to carry a gun, you had best be able to use it or go unarmed.'"

Andrew agreed. "Smart man. You have ammo to reload it?"

"Oh, *sí*. I will clean it first, though, huh?"

"Good idea, but if we're out together on the road, reload it right then. We can clean it later."

"Oh, I see what you mean. I will do that."

"I don't expect us to get in any fights. But the places we'll go are not all nice. We'll have to look out for each other."

"I understand. It is the same in Mexico. Some places have bad ways."

"In two days, I want you to ride with me up to Fort Smith and see about selling them some cattle. Pick a sound horse that you like. We can get him shod. Have a bedroll and be ready to ride."

"*Gracias*, I appreciate this opportunity."

They shook hands. "Oh, you need to come eat with Jackson and me at the house. You can learn more about our business."

"I hope I have manners enough to do that."

"No, just be yourself."

Phil smiled. "I can do that."

Andrew went back to the house and when he stuck his head in, Sophie asked who'd gotten shot.

He chuckled. "That was Philippé showing me he could shoot. He's a good guy. I like him. Hey, if you're choosing me a hat, we need to go to Mason tomorrow."

"I'll be ready early." She sighed like it was a big deal.

"Fine. It was your idea."

"I know. I know." She came out drying her hands. "I think you'll appreciate it. I have those boots done for you, too."

"Can I try them on?"

"That's who I made them for. Come in and do that."

He took a seat on the short bench and wiped his bare feet clean. She gave him the first one. With both hands, he eased his foot into it, then lightly tested its feel on the hard dirt floor.

She handed him the other one. "Now put on this one."

Once on his feet, he stood, doing a short Indian stomp. "They're great. I'll try to get used to wearing them."

"Barefoot ranchers." She shook her head in wonder, laughing softly. "I don't know about you sometimes, boy. But if there's anyplace to sell cattle, I think you'll find it."

"I'm sure going to try."

"No, you'll do it." She touched his arm. "Pride of Texas."

The decided to take Phil along with them on their trip into Mason to buy a hat. Andrew wanted him to get used to being with him and learning his ways. Sophie rode her horse astride, as usual, and sang most of the way, keeping them laughing with her off-color lyrics.

They were about halfway there when she turned serious. She turned to Andrew. "We've got to find Jackson something nice. You're going on a trip and he's staying home."

Andrew considered this. "Well, what does he need?"

It was Phil who came up with the answer. "A bullwhip, *patrón*. Men who can handle one really get good use from it driving cattle and horses."

"It'll keep him busy getting tied up in it." He laughed.

"Good idea." Sophie sounded satisfied. "Bet we can find one."

They found the hat easily. It was a powdery gray, the crown pinched in front and the brim coming down to shade his eyes. Sophie walked around him twice looking it over for color and fit. "That's you, boy."

Andrew looked at it in the hatter's mirror and made a face. He didn't know what to think. It felt... odd. "What does it cost?"

"Damn your hide, Pryor Franks——" she always called him

that when he asked how much something cost, and always with the same scolding expression and tone of voice— "we ain't worrying about *that*. You ever heard how sometimes you got to spend money to make money?"

"Um—no."

"Well, it's true, and you're going to listen to me about it now."

Andrew looked sheepish. "How much?"

"Thirty dollars."

He almost had a heart attack that a *hat* could cost that much. "Twenty-five."

Sophie was already taking a breath. "Pry—"

"I'd do that for you, Mister Franks," the hatter said quickly.

"We'll take it." She cut off the argument with a dark look toward Andrew. Then she dug into her purse and counted out twenty-five silver dollars.

Andrew couldn't miss the look of surprise on the man's face at the cold, hard cash. No doubt he'd expected Confederate trash money. Hell, he might have took less than that if he's known how they'd intended to pay.

But the new hat felt good on his head, there was no denying it. A hell of a lot better than his old beat-up one.

They bought Jackson a bullwhip and a box of .45 bullets for Philippé's pistol. Andrew had .44 balls for his Colt in his saddlebags with the rest of his accessories. Several townspeople told him how good his hat looked. After their rescue of the little girl—Margaret—lots of folks stopped them to talk and see how they were getting along. At the restaurant, the waitresses whistled at his new head cover. They had the lunch special and rode home. Andrew didn't wear his boots. He was saving them for the future.

They had supper that night and talked about the route he should take north. He couldn't get lost, after all. There was a road running all the way to Fort Smith. But if he stayed in the Indian

Territory, he'd have fewer chances of running into any Union soldiers than he would have going through Arkansas.

He would head for San Antonio, then turn north, go through Austin and cross the Brazos at Waco, and ride on. Sophie told him that from there he should go to Fort Worth, then northeast to the Denton Ferry on the Red River. There was a Texas Road went north from there to Fort Smith.

He and Phil had a path to follow and hit it before the sun came up. Jackson'd found him a powerful red roan horse with a swinging gait to match the bay Phil had chosen. With one long-legged, easy-leading packhorse trailing along behind, they made great progress the first day.

When they reached the state capital in Austin, they found people celebrating in the streets. Curious, Andrew asked a well-dressed man in a gray suit what had happened to make everybody so happy. He grinned broadly and threw his beaver hat in the air. The War, by God, he said, was over. General Robert E. Lee had surrendered to the Yankees under General Grant somewhere called Appomattox up in Virginia. They didn't waste any more time listening to all the talk and rumors, but everywhere they went people asked, "You know the war is over?"

When they were finally alone, Andrew let out a long breath. "Thank God. There won't be anyone trying to draft us into the damn army now."

Phil agreed wholeheartedly.

They crossed the Red River north of Denton as planned, paid the black ferryman, then rode off the barge and headed up the hill.

About halfway up, they met a big swarthy-faced man on horseback coming the other direction. He threw them a look of contempt and, as they drew closer, spat on the ground at their feet. "Well, here comes Johnny Reb in his purdy new hat. Hey, boy, speak to me."

Andrew did. He drew his .44 and reined his horse in close.

"I'm only going to speak to you once. I ain't no Johnny Reb, and I'll shoot your ass off right here and now if you say one more word to me. That what you wanted me to say to you?"

"Hell, no."

"Then apologize or you'll be the first man to die in Indian Territory this morning."

The man quickly removed his hat. "I'm sorry."

"Now go mind your own business."

The man hurried on down to the ferry and disappeared from their sight.

Andrew uncocked the pistol and holstered it. "That was a bully about to blossom."

Phil raised his hands, palms out, as though in surrender. "I thought I was supposed to be protecting *you*, *patrón*. It doesn't look to me like you need much protection."

With one final look back, Andrew watched the man climb on board the ferry. Horse's ass. Boy, some folks had their gall. He hoped that was the last one but he knew it wouldn't be.

There would be more people looking for trouble up ahead, he was sure. They had a tough ride ahead of them. Maybe if he was older, there would be less trouble with challenges, but for the moment he didn't give a damn.

He'd take them on as they came.

ELEVEN

THEY STOPPED TO have supper on the mountain where three Indian squaws were busy cooking under some tarps in the post oak forest. Their horses hitched, they walked over to where the older woman collected the money.

"What is there to eat, ma'am?"

"Beef stew, fry bread, and peach cobbler. You have plates?"

Andrew looked back at Phil. "I guess we need our own plates."

The old lady smiled, displaying a mouthful of broken teeth. "Cups, too."

"What does it cost?"

"Ten cents apiece."

Phil went for the horses. "I'll get our stuff."

An Indian family rode up and dismounted. The man paid without a word. Andrew stepped forward and handed over two dimes, then he and Phil followed the others.

A younger Indian woman filled their plates and told them to come back for more and dessert. Another dark-eyed girl took their cups and told them to find a place to sit. She would fill them with coffee and deliver them.

Andrew looked around. The tables scattered about looked

sturdy, and they chose one under a tree in the shade. He hadn't realized just how hungry he was. The last time they'd eaten had been before they'd broken camp that morning. The stew drew saliva at the first hot sip.

He shared a nod with his partner. "We sure stopped at the right place, didn't we, Phil?"

"It's sure better than oatmeal, *patrón.*"

Andrew chuckled. Obviously, Jackson had told the other man about his signature dish. He was never gonna live that down.

The woman who'd taken their coffee cups appeared, holding a steaming mug in each hand. "Where do you live?"

"Near Mason, Texas. Out in the hill country." He pushed his new hat back to take her in. She had dark eyes that danced when she talked. Straight backed, she had a nice figure in the dress—she was near his age and her hair done in thick braids.

"Are you going someplace?"

"Fort Smith. We're looking for markets to sell cattle."

"I wish you good fortune, then. Lots of cattle have gone by here to go somewhere east."

On impulse, he held out his hand. "My name is Andrew. This here is Phil, my partner."

She took his hand in hers. It was very soft. "My name is Yellow Flower."

"Well, um—your food sure is good."

"I do not cook it. I only help to serve it." She smiled shyly, her hands behind her back. "Would you like more?"

"Sure." He rose, plate in hand.

"Good. We like to feed people." She led him back to the large stew pot. An older woman there smiled at him, ready to fill his plate again.

He tossed his head at his man to join him. Phil nodded and hurried over, ready for more, as well. Yellow Flower reminded him to save room for some cobbler and then returned to her duties.

Phil stood at his side, shifting his weight from one foot to the other. "I didn't want to interrupt you and her."

Andrew waved him away. "No problem. She was nice, but I don't really need a woman."

That night, they camped close by and had a breakfast of oatmeal and fried pork for ten cents each. They saw no sign of Yellow Flower again, so they rode on north in the cool morning.

Rain crows cooed, but there were no clouds. The day turned hot, and the horses' hooves churned up clouds of dust around them. In the evening, an angry black cloudbank appeared in the west. Someone was about to get one hell of a storm. Andrew kept an eye on it as they continued on, and Phil agreed they'd see some real hard rain before long.

Soon, they came across a crossroads and what looked like a store and stables. Dismounting and hitching the horses to the post, Andrew hailed one of the loafers sitting on the boardwalk bench watching them.

"Is this a hotel?"

"No." One man shook his head and spat tobacco off the side of the porch.

"We were looking for place to find shelter. Storm's coming."

The man pointed north. "There's a store down the way."

Andrew shrugged and they rode on. "Nice guy, huh?"

Phil laughed. "I guess he didn't want a Mexican and Texan staying there. We might have ruined his sheets."

The rain swept down upon them, erupting out of monstrous lightning and the thunder like cannons in the sky. They were soaked in an instant, pelted with drops the size of silver dollars. They spotted a house a little ways off the road. Someone came to the door and saw them, waved for them to come inside. He and Phil dismounted, hobbled their horses, then ran for the open door. More thunder rolled ominously over the land as they splashed their way up the steps.

A young woman held the door open for them, and offered them each a towel as they fell through it. "That is one bad storm coming. Nobody needs to be out in this."

Andrew's teeth chattered as he used the towel to wipe off his face and hair. "Thanks for rescuing us."

"No need in letting you get blown away." The woman used a towel to ruffle her own wet hair. "Come on in. Find a place."

There were other people and children seated around the room. Most of them were Indians, looking at him curiously in the dim light of a few burning candles. He and Phil removed their hats and nodded their thanks all around.

"We tried to stop at that store," Andrew said. "They told us to move along."

Taking his arm, the young woman guided him to some chairs. "Oh, they're clannish Indians. They don't take very well to outsiders."

"Are we safe here?"

"As safe as we can be, I guess. We don't have a cellar."

He pointed toward the thundering hail. "Well, we sure appreciate the roof."

"My name is Myshell."

"This is Phil. I'm Andrew."

"Where are you boys headed?"

"Fort Smith."

"Is the war really over? Have you heard?"

"Yes, ma'am. The war is over."

An enormous crash of thunder sounded right above their heads. She gasped, startled, and fell against him.

Unsure of just exactly what to do, especially in a room full of people, Andrew held her very lightly and helped her stand.

In the light of the candles, her face had turned bright red. "I'm so sorry. I'm not usually so clumsy."

"Nothing to apologize for. Hell, that made *me* jump."

She smiled, her eyes searching his. "Please sit down, Andrew. I'm very glad to meet you."

"Yes, ma'am. We're grateful you invited us inside."

"No problem. Do you have a wife?"

"Oh, no."

"What a shame." She moved on to answer a baby crying in some woman's arms.

The storm settled down into hard, steady rain and he sat in the wooden chair with his elbows on his knees. Sure nice to get out of the weather. Tough to have been caught out in it. Lucky there was no twister in this one. He'd grown up with tornados in north Arkansas that occasionally ripped away all people had and spread it out.

Later, he found Myshell again and offered her a few dollars for inviting them inside. She shook her head and pushed it away. "You could stay here overnight if you like. It would be dry to sleep out in my barn. It's right out back."

"We need to find our horses."

"I have a candle lamp. You can borrow it."

"The lamp might help."

"I'll go get it."

In a short while, they found the horses close by. They were soaked, but otherwise uninjured. Myshell showed them to the barn. He handed her the lamp, and she asked him to bend down. He did, and she kissed him—*hard*.

He wasn't sure what to do. So he kissed her harder and then they stood there, him holding her ripe body against his own. His heart beat like a drum in his chest. He felt the urgent need to hold her, have her, like he'd never felt before.

"If you need me, I'm here, big man."

And with that, she took the lamp and left.

He didn't fall asleep for a very long time, indeed.

TWELVE

AT DAWN, MYSHELL served them breakfast and coffee. It wasn't Arbuckle coffee, but the German fried potatoes, eggs, bacon, and biscuits tasted like heaven after a damp night in the barn. They squatted beside the house to eat and thanked her most kindly. She had a coffee pot ready to refill their cups.

Offhand, Andrew would guess her to be in her twenties. She had eyes that were big, dark, and intense above a mouth of straight, white teeth. Her hair was long and glossy black, and as soft to the touch as her skin. And her bosom... well, there was a reason he had problems looking her in the eye.

She was very concerned about them and their welfare. "You should stay a few days. It's storm season, you could get caught out in the weather again."

He sighed. "I'm sorry, Myshell. I have business to attend to. Then I have to go home."

She dropped her gaze and looked hurt.

But Andrew didn't know what else to say. He couldn't stay. Jackson and Sophie were depending on him, and they'd worked too hard for him to just abandon them and everything they'd built together.

He sighed.

They finished their food, thanked her, and then handed back her plates, silverware, and cups. Then they mounted up and rode off.

When they were out of sight, Philippé turned to him and grinned. "I think she wanted you to stay with her, *patrón*"

"I told you. I don't need a wife."

"She cooked good food."

"I don't need a good cook, either."

He had business ahead, he hoped, and that was the important thing. And it would be good to get back to business. Yet the entire incident gnawed at him. For some reason, he felt at once like he'd barely escaped, but also that he'd missed out on something that could have been very special.

They crossed the Canadian River and rode east under directions from the ferryman. There was a lot of road traffic headed the same way they were. When they finally reached the banks of the Arkansas, Fort Smith spread out before them on the other side—a bustling collection of red-brick buildings clustered along both sides of a wide dirt street.

They took the ferry over and rode down Garrison Avenue. At the stables, the liveryman warned them the law took a dim view of men wearing their guns out in the open. Not wanting any trouble, they rolled up their holsters and belts, and stuck them deep down in their saddlebags.

"Your things will be safe here," the man promised.

They set out to find a meal. As they walked, more than a few loafers made comments about the barefoot hick and his spic. With an effort, Andrew ignored them. They were in a new country and needed no problem with the law. But it was a hell of a challenge not to stand up to.

They entered a café and woman's wide smile welcomed them as she showed them to a clean table.

"We have pork roast, potatoes, fresh green beans, and coffee."

"That all sounds great."

She smiled. "You boys must be new in town."

"Yes, ma'am. We came to sell some cattle."

"Good luck. People drive cattle in here all the time. I guess they sell them here."

"That's what we need. A cattle buyer."

They had just tucked into their meals when a man in a brown suit stopped at their table. "Did I overhear you gents say you were looking to sell some cattle?"

Andrew swallowed and rose to shake the man's hand. "My name's Andrew Franks. I'm looking for a market for some cattle."

"Tyrone Gipson. I buy cattle. Do you have a herd here?"

"No, sir, but I can get them here."

"Here's my card. Come by my office at the stockyards. We'll talk turkey."

Andrew waved the card at him. "Thanks, we'll sure do that."

"Good day."

He smiled down at Phil, then took his place again. "Well, we have a lead."

"And we've only been here ten minutes." Phil took a sip of his coffee. "Not bad food. And no oatmeal. We need to remember this place."

This tickled Andrew. "We've definitely had worse."

They paid fifteen cents apiece for the meal and headed back out onto the street.

This place was a wonder. Neither of them was used to tall buildings, and Fort Smith had a few blocks of them. There were women in slatted bonnets, women wearing fancy hats, and others bare-headed. They came in all shapes and forms.

He recognized some fancy doves in low-cut gowns selling their wares on the street and they about embarrassed him. He knew awfully little about females, even after his months with

Sophie, but if he were being truthful, the sight of those girls was more than slightly tempting. Especially when he remembered how he'd felt when Myshell had kissed him two nights before.

They found Gipson at his office at the stockyards, hard by the river. He gave them a tour, walking them up and down through the almost endless pens, talking all the while. He stopped to show them some fat steers all bunched in one lot. The big five-year-old slick steers eyed them warily and tossed long horns their way.

"See how slick and fat they are?" Gipson pointed. "Those're top steers, boys. They'll bring the most money in any market. Let's look at the next pen."

Andrew looked over the lean, younger longhorns gathered there. They looked gaunt—almost skeletal. He glanced up at Gipson in concern. "Someone actually brought these to market?"

The cattle buyer nodded. "Yes, sir. They're near worthless, but they brought them anyway. Now I'll need to fatten them up to make anything at all off them. You got any big steers in Texas like those ones I just showed you?"

He nodded. "Yes, sir, I do. How much are they worth?"

"Forty dollars a head if they're that good."

"How many could you use?"

"Oh, two hundred."

That made him smile. "I can't drive that few steers up here."

"Oh?" Now the man seemed interested. "What's the smallest herd you could bring?"

"Five hundred."

"That would be lots of cattle for me to handle, but I might be able to split them up. "

Andrew considered this, running numbers in his head. Thank God for Sophie and her multiplication tables.

He could buy steers in Texas for ten to twelve dollars a head. That and the food bill, plus horses and men would run them close to fifteen hundred dollars. Of course, some would be their own branded steers, but he doubted that they had over a hundred fifty of them that good. He'd need good ones. That would cost him— call it four thousand dollars.

Then they'd be two months or longer on the road to drive them up here. Even with the *vaqueros'* payroll, that would run a hundred twenty dollars or more depending on conditions they found on the way.

So, all together it would cost him about five thousand to make it happen.

Gipson was giving him the eye. "What do you think?"

Andrew played it close to the vest. "That cuts any money I could make as close."

The cattle buyer shrugged. "It's a risky business, all right. You've seen what I need, and you strike me as someone with an eye for cattle. When do you think you could you get them here?"

"Three months."

"So fall?"

"Yes, sir."

"You can let me know the details if you accept my offer."

He nodded. "Thank you. I *do* see what you want. And I understand. If I can make money, I'll sure do it."

They shook hands.

Andrew liked the man, but he had not heard from the competition yet. Only a fool jumped at the first offer he could find. There were others in the business he wanted to talk to, as well.

As they headed back toward downtown, they were forced to dodge all sorts of crowds. There were lots of blue coat soldiers galloping about through traffic like they were on a mission—real important-like. There were plenty of gray and butternut uniforms milling around, as well. The war might be over now, but parts about it damn sure weren't.

Tribesmen loafed around wrapped in blankets, being waited on by squaws. Most drank pints of beer—illegal. Indians weren't supposed to be able to buy liquor, but they found ways to, or at least traded for it. Their small children looked hard-eyed at the white men and women. Dispersed in the sidewalk traffic, he had to be careful where he stepped around them on the sidewalk.

From nowhere, a burly guy suddenly busted into him, knocking him to the ground.

"Watch yourself, hick."

Andrew scrambled to his feet, his fists clenched. "Who the hell you calling a hick?"

"You, you barefoot hillbilly. Keep out of my gawdamn way."

"Step aside."

"Oh, yeah? And what are you going to do about it?"

Abruptly, the man bolted upright. Andrew looked at him in confusion for a moment until Phil peeked out from behind the big clog, smiling broadly. Obviously, his partner had a knife against the man's spine.

Andrew grinned, looked up at the man with a sneer. "Maybe my friend'll cut your kidney out, huh?"

"You two'll be in jail 'fore you get the horseshit out from between your toes."

Andrew got in his face. "Apologize."

"We meet again, you better be armed." Pain from Phillipé's knife changed his plea and he dropped to his knees. "I'm sorry, mister. I'm *sorry*!"

"What's your name?" Andrew demanded

"Garth Pool."

"Mind your own business next time and I'll mind mine, Pool."

The man made a face, then sprawled on his belly in the dirt moaning. The knife must have been stuck in him.

Philippé wiped the blade off on his pants and returned it to the sheath. "He won't die."

"Good thing. We need to find a better part of town."

They made it back in the business district when another

man, this one closer to his own age, came out of a saloon and tried to pick a fight with the barefoot cowboy. He made one rush at Andrew, swinging his fists, before ending up busted on his ass rubbing his jaw. He got all he wanted from the new guy in town.

"Maybe I should wear my new boots here, huh?" He pushed on west with no place to go.

Phil sounded unconcerned."It wasn't that. Maybe something you said, huh? He doesn't like oatmeal, maybe."

They reached the stable, where the owner let them sleep in the hay to save room costs. They were unrolling their bedrolls when an older man came over and introduced himself as Johnny Hazelton—cattle buyer.

"You boys have any cattle on the road now?"

"No, but I could raise some at home and drive them up here—if you've got the market and the price is right."

They squatted down in the shade of the alleyway. A stiff breeze out of the south swept Andrew's sweaty face as he listened to the well-dressed older man under the narrow-brimmed Stetson.

"They have to be big steers. How many can you drive up here at a time?"

"I figure four, five hundred."

"When can they be here?"

"Three months."

"That would be winter time here."

"Yes. What could you pay for them?"

"Forty bucks, if they're fat."

Same number. Five hundred cattle at forty a head would bring in twenty thousand dollars, minus the five thousand to buy the rest he needed, feed them, and drive them up here. But if they didn't bring forty a head, he might lose his ass. "Since you sound so honest and really want them, I know what you need—fat cattle, four and five years old. I think I know how to get them here fat. I need to trail four hundred head up here to make profit."

Green agreed. "You want to shake on that deal?"

Andrew agreed and they shook hands. He had a cattle deal. Now he had to make it work.

"Tell me something, Mr. Hazelton?"

"Go ahead."

"I've been in almost three scrapes today. Are all these guys my age itching for a fight?"

The man shook his head. "Ah hell, they lost a war and want to win one for a change. You'll bring four hundred head of fat beeves up here in three months—I'll get you forty dollars a head for them and they can all go to hell."

"How do I find you?"

The man gave him his business card. His office was in the First Bank Building. Impressed, Andrew tucked it away to keep. Then they shook his hands again on the deal. "Four hundred at forty bucks?"

"That's my deal."

"I'll be in touch."

"How're you going to keep them fat coming up here?" Phil asked when they were alone.

"Corn'll be cheap. We came by lots of it still in the fields. Ear corn will be ten cents a bushel this fall. If I can feed them four to five pounds the last thirty days on the road, they'll be fat as pigs. Cost me ninety dollars or so for the corn. I have two wagons at home we can use to transport it."

"What can you buy steers for?"

"I can't pay over ten bucks a head for them."

"You think people will sell them to you for that?"

"I don't know." He shrugged. "We better hurry home, though. We have lots to do."

"We better, hadn't we?"

"You don't have time to fight these crazy guys, either."

Andrew agreed about that fighting business. "We'll go home

and tell the rest. It's five hundred sixty miles from San Antonio to here. That's thirty-seven days if we have no problems on the way."

"How did you figure that so fast?"

He chuckled. "Sophie has us solve all kinds of number problems. That's coming fifteen miles a day. Take you and me two weeks to get back home if we hurry. Then we have to buy steers. Then we'll be busy getting horses ready, teams ready, *us* ready."

They rode through more than a few thunderstorms going home, but made it on his time schedule. The storms were a good thing—moisture would make more pasture for his stock going north. When they got two weeks north of San Antonio they'd need to start feeding them corn every day, and they'd likely pass rustling dry cornfields on the ride home. Who would be his corn buyer and keep them in grain? They'd need some teams to pull those two farm wagons. His mind ran wild.

He could get fifty or sixty bushels of corn in a wagon bed. That meant they could only hold three to four days' supply of corn per wagon, so in a week they'd eat both loads and need more. He would need eight more wagonloads to get there. Maybe his plan was too farfetched, but that was what he'd needed.

Farmers were poor that year, so he could hire some to haul it for him and meet up with him at certain points on the road. It would cost, but if this plan worked he might have a good enough idea how to make real money at it.

Back at the Turkey Track, he found Jackson chomping at the bit and Sophie ready for a rest away from him. Andrew immediately sat them down and sketched out his plan for them, with Phil adding details as to how it all would work.

Jackson scratched his chin. "Sounds tough, but we can try it."

The next three weeks were a damn blur.

Jackson's *vaqueros* went south and brought back over two hundred head on consignment from the small Mexican ranchers south of them. While they'd been gone, Jackson and one of the other hands had fixed the old wagons, put big sides on them, and found mule teams to rent for the trip. Sophie declared she'd be going along to cook for them, so they had bought her a buckboard for her to bring her things in and a light team to pull it.

Andrew and Phil rode on up the road to buy corn along the way. They met with some success and had the loads lined up. Back at the ranch, Jackson supervised the road branding of the herd and got them all ready to move out.

Many folks around those parts shook their heads at the idea of their leaving in late summer like that. Plumb foolish, they called it. Why, they might get snowed in up there at Fort Smith, and then what would they do? On top of that, what was this rumor about them feeding longhorns corn on the trail to fatten them? Nobody had ever heard of anything like that, either. Foolishness.

Andrew stuck to his guns, though, and stayed the course. This was his plan, and by God, he'd see it through.

Of course, the trip wasn't without its scary moments.

On the first night out, the steers had shown no interest at all in the corn. These were dry ears in the husk left on the ground. The cattle had damn sure never eaten much nor seen the like before, and they left a great trail of corn to move up in a large circle and graze, instead. Andrew had gone to sleep with nightmare visions of rolling into Fort Smith with four hundred head of walking longhorn skeletons like Mr. Gipson had shown him in the stockyards.

By day four, though, the steers were bawling for the corn, and were the most content longhorns he'd ever seen or driven, chomping down on whole ears and licking the grain off the dirt.

His wagon system worked out fine, too, between their two wagons and the two farmers he'd found from up near Dennison. Eric Holder and Clyde Martin had put up lots of corn and welcomed a buyer who wasn't worried about the grade.

The rest of the drive passed smoothly. They had no trouble

with Indians or outlaws, and crossed the shallow Canadian thirty-five days out of San Antonio. They'd even be there early.

Using the steam ferry, Andrew and Phil rode on ahead into town. It was a cool mid-morning in mid-November, and Fort Smith was awake. So was their buyer.

"I've been hearing about you coming for weeks. Some crazy Texas cowboys driving steers and feeding them corn."

Andrew grinned lopsidedly. "Wait till you see them. They're fat and licking their hair in circles."

"You're early, but I can still use them. Let's go look."

"That's what we came for. That feeding them costs money. We need to sell them."

On the ferry ride back over, Andrew explained what he'd done. Hazelton shook his head, impressed with the young man and his manner. "Forget that you don't wear boots, son. I think I'm talking to one of the future great cattle barons of Texas."

"I don't know about that, but we have the whole outfit here today, my brother Jackson included."

It didn't take more than a second for Hazelton to see the quality of the steers before him. His jaw dropped in disbelief. "These may be the best-looking steers I've ever seen. I'm going to try to get you forty-five dollars a head, and make them pay me my commission. They are *that* good."

Andrew didn't mind hearing that at all. "We can use it. We lost two on the trip, so we have four hundred and five head total."

"They'll talk about them in town tomorrow. I'm impressed as I can possibly be. I'll have buyers here by tomorrow afternoon." They shook hands and their cattle buyer hurried back to town before the sun went down.

In camp, Sophie had her lamp on while she worked out their expenses. Food, miscellaneous costs, and corn costs amounted to $250. The *vaqueros* cost fifteen bucks a month, so close to a hundred dollars for the six men's wages for the drive. They'd bought a hundred head of steers at ten bucks. Fifty of the herd were their own cattle. The rest they'd brought on consignment. The next Monday, Hazelton handed them a check for $18,260.00. For the 250 head that came from the small Mexican ranchers and others, Andrew, Jackson, and Sophie had agreed to pay them $25 a head.

With all the expenses taken into account, they'd made over nine thousand dollars.

Sophie showed them the final figures. "I told you boys you would be cattle barons."

That afternoon they bathed and changed into their Sunday best. Sophie had even brought a new dress along to wear. They went to town and ate supper at The Fairmont House Restaurant in the Ascot Hotel.

Besides his new pants, Andrew wore his new boots. After they finished their meals, they even bought Jackson a new hat.

They paid their *vaqueros* and gave them each a five-dollar bonus. Whooping with joy, half of them headed into town to celebrate. The other half watched the camp, horses, and supplies. There were too many thieves in the area to leave things unguarded. But the boys promised the hands on watch the chance to go into town and raise some hell the next night before they headed home.

Standing outside their sidewall tent under the stars, Jackson shook his head. "You know, them gawdamn wagons never got stuck once coming up here. Not one time. Remember going to Texas, they were stuck all the time?"

Andrew also recalled they didn't need the old man's bitching and beating on them to get there, either. He clapped his brother on the shoulder and wished him a good night.

What next? Go to this Abilene, Kansas place he'd heard about with a herd? That might be next. He'd had a taste of making money at cattle drives now. He smiled and wondered what that woman who'd kissed him on the mountain might think now if she knew about his success.

THIRTEEN

SABRINA, WHO HAD watched the ranch with a skeleton crew, said no one came around while they were gone. It had been very quiet—almost too much so. This was the time of year the Comanche finished hunting and made raids on western Texas outposts during the full moons. Andrew warned everyone to be on the lookout for barefoot pony tracks and scattered horse droppings. A range mustang always stopped to poop. Indians riders never let their horses stop.

He made the rounds with Phil to all the small ranchers who had sent cattle along with them. To a man, they were all very excited and pledged more cattle to sell when he went again. He told them he'd be in touch. These people, his neighbors. had few outlets to sell stock for cash. The largest of them had sent eight steers, the rest only handfuls, but they had trusted him and he hadn't let them down. And they'd saved his ass in doing so.

They were invited to a celebration in a small community nearby. It was nighttime and dark. One girl danced and clacked her castanets in the firelight. Her beauty was serpent-like in the buckskin dress, and her willowy figure wove a dreamy pattern in the glow of the fire.

Andrew fell captivated.

Phil nudged him with his elbow. "You want to meet her?"

"What, you know her?"

"All my life." He grinned. "Her name is Tasha. Her father is a rancher, Eliza Miguel. We didn't sell any of his cattle this time, but he spoke to me about the next time."

"Does she have any suitors?"

The *vaquero* looked at him like he was crazy. "Of course."

"What would I do? What would I say to her?"

"Oh, you *gringos*." Phil shook his head. "Trust me, you'll find your tongue. You can talk to anyone. I've seen you do it."

"I am proud of your faith in me. Maybe later."

"Don't complain later. I tried."

He clapped him on the shoulder. "You do a good job watching my back. Thanks, anyway."

They went off to sleep in their bedrolls. He just about had everyone paid except for two other families they planned to get to in the morning. It was a warm night and the crickets were loud. Somewhere a coyote yapped mournfully and a great owl made a low pass over the camp, his silent wings lifting him higher.

Andrew's sleep was not so peaceful, however. His dreams were filled with images of Comanche braves, sweeping out of the brush and running them down in the bloody night. He awoke with a start, covered in sweat, Colt in hand, searching the starlit campsite.

But he found nothing.

What the hell?

Once, there had been such an attack on the ranch, just a few months after they'd arrived. Pa had seen the signs warning of a coming raid, though, and was ready for them. They'd killed four warriors in an all-out, night-long gun and arrow exchange. The war party finally left at dawn, but Pa had claimed they took other dead ones with them. Being a kid, Andrew had believed him. But there had been no letup in the hell of their screaming and bitter gun smoke that had filled the small house all through the night before.

Andrew holstered his gun again and settled back into his bedroll. Had the dream been an omen of some kind? A forewarning? He wasn't certain, but he'd damn sure be on watch from now on—just in case.

The next morning, the local families served him and Phil breakfast. Andrew had just taken his first bite of an enormous burrito when he looked up and found himself looking into the eyes of the girl from the night before.

He nearly choked trying to swallow that unchewed bite.

"*Señor* Franks, I am so sorry I did not get to meet you last night." She swept her dress under her legs and took a place close to where he sat. "My name is—"

"Tasha Miguel." He coughed, cleared his throat. "My— my *compadre* told me last night. You dance very well."

She blushed. "And your name is Andrew Franks?"

"That's right."

"You have helped out many of my neighbors selling their cattle up there. We are all very grateful."

Frazzled, Andrew took a drink of coffee to play for time. "We did well that trip. Lots of work, but in the end it worked out well."

"How did you think of all that?"

"There was a large Texas corn crop. I rode by fields of it going up there. I knew five pounds of corn a day would fatten anything."

"But to feed and move them?"

He laughed. "All of us got new muscles shoveling it out."

"How did you get them to eat it?"

"The first night they walked through lots of it. I thought they would ignore it, but they discovered it and then we were in shape to make the drive."

"Sounds very wild. You fed them every day?"

"Every day."

"It worked?"

"Oh, he wanted more cattle like them. But I didn't think we could do that again. Those big steers have all been driven north. I found out fast there aren't many of them left. Having the corn—I had two great ranchers helping me. Up in Indian Territory, we had to bring it along with us. But it all worked. We had corn every day."

He stopped. Was this divine creature really interested in the boring details of a cattle drive? Or was she trying to get him talking for some other reason.

"How far is that?"

"Um... from our place to San Antonio six hundred miles to Fort Smith, I would say."

"Eat." She giggled and gestured toward his forgotten breakfast. "It is better hot than cold."

He shrugged "I guess I could talk all day about the trip." He took another bite, watching her out of the corner of his eye. Damn, she was beautiful.

"How did you come to hire all these *vaqueros*?"

"Well, actually, my brother, Jackson, found them at first. He hired them to catch wild horses—um, mustangs. They're all great hard workers, so we kept them on."

"There is not much work in this area. We all appreciate that they have work and that you treat them fair."

"Good, we love them."

"Will you make another drive?"

He wiped his mouth on the back of hand. "Phil and I talked about that this morning. We may go to Abilene next spring."

"Will you take more of my people's cattle?"

"Oh, yes."

"Good." She fixed him with those sparkling brown eyes and maybe the sweetest smile he'd ever seen. "I must go. My father is waiting for me. But it has been a pleasure to meet you. You must come by our ranch at Blanco Springs. You are invited."

He rose when she did and nearly tripped. "I'll be by."

She smiled again. "Splendid. I am counting on that visit."

He watched the swing of her slender hips as she hurried away. What a nice young woman.

Philippé broke his concentration with a smug smile. "See? I told you you could talk to her. Thank God you weren't eating oatmeal. Your jaws may have gotten stuck together."

"*You* did that!"

The *vaquero* looked at him innocently. "Did what?"

"You brought her over here to meet me."

"Only because you were too *tímido* to do it yourself." He laughed. "Besides, she asked me to."

Andrew's eyes got big as silver dollars. "She did?"

"She wanted to meet *el patrón,* the local cattle baron. How could I say no to my childhood friend?"

"I really hate when people call me that." He sat back down and picked at the remains of the burrito.

"But that's what you are, *mano*. It's not a bad thing. It's like a— how you say, a patriarch? The head of the family that takes care of everyone. That's something to be proud of. Especially at your age."

Philippé was right. That's what he did, all right. But he felt like letting people call him *patrón* was... arrogant or something. He wasn't above anyone. He was just trying to make a go of it for his family.

His thoughts turned back to Tasha. She had taken him by surprise. She was beautiful, smart and—mature. Not like most girls around his age. He would go by to see her and her father later in the year, like she'd asked.

He wanted a plan to take cattle to Kansas first, though.

LIKE ALWAYS, THE gears in his head were turning. A trip to Kansas would take a hell of a lot of planning. There must be a good, well planned deal first and something that would earn them money—they didn't need a hot summer spent driving cattle up there and come home empty-handed.

There had been many bad deals he'd heard about. Herds lost or stolen by outlaws, men robbed of the proceeds coming home. Wrecks and cyclones, the drowning of many animals at river crossings. One guy got all his neighbors' cattle up there, sold them, and disappeared with the money, never to be heard of again. All things he wanted to avoid.

But never having been there, he had lots to learn.

He'd heard of a man named Caleb Jessup who lived near Fredericksburg who'd made several successful drives to Abilene. He'd try and find him when he got the time.

Later in the morning, he and Phil rode down a narrow canyon lined with live oak, headed for the next-to-last family they owed money to. The back of his neck itched as he rode along. Something wasn't quite right here. With his hand on his gun butt, he kept his head on a swivel. He'd never met these people they were headed for. One of the *vaqueros* had talked them into putting their steers in the drive.

He breathed a little easier when the way opened up and the ranch headquarters was in sight. Dogs barked, small children pointed at them, and a woman with a rifle went and put it up on the porch.

Obviously, he wasn't the only one anxious around here.

"Missus Rodriguez?"

"*Sí.*"

He dropped out of the saddle. "I'm Andrew Franks, and I have money here for you for your cattle."

The woman swept her hair back and smiled. "That is very good. We can always use money, *señor.*"

"You sent five steers with us to Arkansas. I'm paying one hundred and twenty-five dollars for those cattle."

"Oh, I heard they did well. That will help us all here." She looked ready to cry as he put the money in her hand.

"I plan another drive next year. I'll come back and talk to your husband when we get ready to go."

She sniffed. "Oh, yes, he will be ready. This helps so much."

Andrew looked around. The itch on the back of his neck hadn't gone away yet. "Aren't you afraid of Comanche living down here?"

She nodded. "Them and border bandits both."

"Is your man due back soon?"

"Any day. I'd hoped you were him."

"Stay safe, ma'am. And thank you."

"God be with you, *señor*. This was a very good thing for us." She held up the money in the leather pouch.

He remounted, waved, and he and Phil rode back down the narrow way back to the open country.

He shuddered. "Spooky place to live."

"I thought so too. I had heard of them but never had been there before." Phil twisted in the saddle and looked back at the mountains. "I'm glad we're out of there in one piece."

"Amen."

They reached the Ronaldo Baca Ranch in late afternoon. The RBR was a small ranch, set up beside a large spring tank in the flatter country. Baca had consigned eight head to him. He owed him two hundred dollars.

They were breaking horses in a dusty pen. Baca was a short man who came out the corral brushing away dust and pulling off his gloves. His face was dark and his mustache long, he had a wide smile for him.

"You must be Ronaldo Baca. I'm Andrew Franks. I owe you some money for your eight steers."

"I heard you made it up there. Lots of good talk. I wondered if I needed to go over to your ranch to collect."

"Not at all. I have two hundred dollars here for you. We did all right at Fort Smith. No real problems on the trail."

"That is great to hear. When will you go back?"

"Maybe Kansas in the spring. Do you think you might have some cattle to go with us then?"

Baca thought about it for a moment. "If I had a hundred, could you take them?"

"If I go up there, yes."

"Let us drink some coffee in the shade. This is wonderful news. But a good drive of a hundred would really help the small outfits around here like me."

"It'll help us all. That's why we do it."

Baca led them around the house to a covered porch. His wife—he introduced her as Theresa, and she was visibly pregnant—brought them all coffee. Andrew took a sip and recognized it immediately as Arbuckle's. No doubt she'd saved it for company.

After some more small talk, Andrew handed over the canvas pouch containing *Señor* Baca's profits.

Baca opened the pouch and his eyes got wide. He shook the heavy canvas bag and the coins jingled inside. "It's all in silver!"

He nodded. "Yes, sir. The war's over, finally. Confederate money's no good anymore."

The little rancher found this hilarious. "Well, good. I didn't have any, anyway."

"You're breaking horses today I see?" Andrew motioned toward the pens.

"*Sí.* You have a market for them, too?"

"Sometimes I can sell them in Fort Worth."

"What are they worth?"

"Good geldings fifteen at my place."

"My boys and I have a hard time finding horse buyers. A trip to San Antonio hardly pays our expenses. I pick out sharp horses to break. I can show you some." He looked to his wife. "Have Don bring up two good horses on leads for this man to look at."

"Yes, but you will have to pour your own coffee." She winked and disappeared into the house.

"It is hard to make a living out here." Baca shook his head, then raised his cup in both hands for another sip.

Soon a boy of fourteen or so led two good horses up for their inspection. One was gray, and had such clear eyes and pride in his posture, Andrew liked him on sight. The other one was a light buckskin with lots of muscle. The wind tossed their manes and they had deep-throated calls to their separated *compadres*. Andrew lifted up front hooves and inspected their teeth.

Damn fine horses.

"I may lose my backside, but off the hoof, I'd offer you twenty apiece for them."

"Sold!"

Phil nodded in approval. They were exceptional horses and he said so privately to Andrew.

"If you have more, send them to me, Baca. I can split what they make with you."

"Good. There will be more."

They politely turned down his offer to stay the night. Andrew paid him for the horses and they headed for home.

Andrew could hardly believe his purchases. They'd never had horses of such quality on the ranch before. When they got home, he'd give Jackson his choice. The buckskin was powerfully built, but the gray was a handsome lot and had plenty of muscles to rope off of, too.

They finally made camp at sundown, ate some jerky, and turned in. Then they were in the saddle again before dawn, headed for the ranch.

He planned to sleep a few days once they got back.

It came as a shock when he rode into the homestead and caught sight of the new house for the first time. The walls of the rambling new *hacienda* were all laid out and now chest high. He couldn't believe how far it had come in such a short time—nor how big it was. He found Jackson in the dooryard, shading his eyes from the morning sun and examining the two new horses.

"Where did you steal them?"

"You *do* know we don't have to do that anymore, right?"

"Yeah, I just like to think of my big brother as the outlaw type." Jackson grinned. "You cut quite the figure in your boots and hat, you know."

Typical Jackson. "I bought them for us from Ronaldo Baca. Take your pick and it's yours. I'll take the other one."

His brother stomped around, checking their teeth and legs.

Sophie appeared in the doorway to the house and rushed out to him. "Andrew!"

"Hey, Sophie."

"It's so good to have you home. I was about to send the *federales* out to look for you if you didn't show up soon." She wrapped him in a bear hug. "Did you get new horses?"

"Yep. He's making his choice now. It may take a while."

"Ha! Buckskin!" Jackson waved his arms. "You're not the only one who can make a quick decision, Mister Big-Shot Rancher."

Sophie walked over and ran a hand down the silky nose of the grey. The horse nuzzled her back gently. "They're beautiful. Don't tell me, you wanted the grey, right?"

He nodded.

She laughed merrily. "He looked like a big rancher's horse to me, all right."

His arm on her shoulder, Andrew lowered his voice. "Sophie, how many more Mexicans did you hire to work on the new house after we got back?"

"Four." She twisted to see his face. "Is that okay? Jackson told me I could do it."

He waved it away. "No problem. Its size just shocked me."

"Big ranchers need big houses to entertain in."

He nodded, squeezed her shoulder, then followed her inside the old house.

Leaning against the back of one of the kitchen chairs, she watched him take off his gun belt, hat, and bandana. "So... what's next?"

"A bath, shave, and three days' sleep."

"I'll have Sabrina get the boys to heat up some bath water. I bet you can't sleep over one day, though."

"No bet. I'll try."

"We'll need another well dug here soon. I fear we use too much water and this one may go dry."

"More money. It's always more money." He sighed. "Who witches wells around here, anyway?"

"Raul says there's a girl somewhere down south. Tasha, or something like that."

That brought his head around. "Tasha? *Really*?" A *witch*?

Sophie smiled slyly. She didn't miss anything. "I take it you know her?"

"Um, well... maybe." With as hot as his face had gotten, he was sure he must've just turned about four shades of red. "Sort of."

"You dog. And here I thought you were down there paying off all of our benefactors."

He licked his lips. "I was."

"Uh-huh." The smile grew wider. "But I guess you found some time to be social, too, huh? Mister Big-Shot Rancher."

"I saw her dance at a celebration they had, that's all."

"Uh-huh...."

"Philippé has known her since they were children. He says she asked about me, so he introduced us."

"Is she pretty?"

"Beautiful." Andrew sighed, then caught himself. He turned around. "I tripped all over myself talking to her. Nearly choked to death on a damn burrito, too. I don't know a thing about women, Sophie."

"Well, why don't we invite her out here to find us a well?" She walked over and put her arm around his shoulders. "If you're nice, maybe I can even give you some lessons in talking to the fairer sex without getting tongue-tied."

"When am I ever not nice?"

"Well," she said innocently. "The guys in Fort Smith certainly didn't seem to like you."

"I meant to you."

"I know what you meant." She grinned and rubbed his arm. "You've got it bad, huh?"

"I don't know what I've got, Sophie. I haven't exactly been very successful with women so far."

"That's just because you haven't been around very many besides me. We'll have to change that. Besides—" her smile broadened, "—if you like her as much as it sounds like, it should come fairly easy."

"That's the thing. I don't really know what I like, or even what I *feel*." He fell down into one of the chairs. "What we're doing here—for us, our family—is important. I don't need any distractions. Especially when I don't know what she really wants. Me, or what she thinks I might become. It's like Pa. He didn't give a shit about me or Jackson. He only cared what he could use us for."

"Oh, sweetheart." Sophie squatted down beside him and pulled his head down to her chest. "You don't know that. You can't. You're so smart, so strong, you can't go through the rest of your life looking at everyone and seeing your father."

"It *is* hard." He sniffled, wiped his nose. "You're the first person to ever treat us like *people*, Sophie. Like we're worth something. It didn't matter that we didn't know our numbers, or didn't have nice clothes, you believed in us. But you're the only one. Nobody else liked us until after we started making any money in business."

And that was it. Truth be told, Tasha made him uncomfortable, and not for the reason Sophie thought. To him, Tasha acted like a woman with a purpose. If he invited her here, he'd be in her debt. Why did that make him uneasy? Because he'd lose control of how things progressed? Was he afraid of her? Maybe he saw too much. They were only talking about a damn well, weren't they? Really? How involved could *that* be?

"Andrew, that's the kindest thing anybody has ever said to me."

"It's true." He hung his head. "But what I can't figure is why you did it."

"Why I did what?"

"Why'd you come here to take care of us—why you love and believe in Jackson and I so much after... after what Pa did to you up in Arkansas."

Her arms around him went rigid. "What?"

"C'mon, Sophie. You know what I'm talking about."

"What I mean is how do *you* know what he did?"

"It's in your voice whenever we talk about him. Whenever we talk about moving here, about passing through Yell County, there's something you hold back. Something you don't tell us." He looked up into her eyes. "He hurt you, didn't he? Pa. The way men do to women."

"Oh, God, Andrew, we don't need to talk about this now."

"You don't have to talk about it. I *know*, Sophie. And I hate him more for it than I ever did when he was alive."

"Andrew...."

"But how can you do what you do for me and Jackson? Just tell me that. We're his *sons*. Aren't you afraid—"

"No. Never." Smiling sadly, she reached up and wiped her own tears away. "You're not him. Is that what you're worried about? You're *you*, Andrew, and I love you for that alone. You're nothing like your father. Neither is your brother. Pryor could never have done anything like you boys have done, even in the short time I've been here. That's why I call you by his name when I see you doing something he did. Because you're better than that. You boys are good and kind young men. You're smart and you work hard, and you take care of each other and the people you love. I could see that even when you were twelve. *That's* why I came here, even after what he did. And I've never regretted it for even a second."

"I think you're the best person I've ever met."

"But I can't be."

"Why not?"

"Because you are."

They held each other like that for while longer, gently wiping away one another's tears while the ranch work continued outside. Eventually, they put themselves back together. Sophie went back out to the cook shack, and Andrew headed off to bathe, shave, and catch a nap in a hammock in the shade.

JACKSON CAME AND woke him sometime later.

"Hey. I need some help."

"What's that?" Andrew wrung out his face with his calloused palms and sat up. His senses were slow to recover.

"Are we really going to Kansas next year?"

He yawned. "I've told some we might. What have you got?"

"I think we should hire some more *vaqueros* and get busy branding mavericks. There's going to be a lot of soldiers coming back from war looking for a way to make a living. If we can do it, what makes us think they can't? We need to get the jump on them and get all we can, while we can. What do you think?"

"I... guess we should hire some more *vaqueros* and brand as many as we can."

"I'm making us a chuckwagon like the one we saw going to Fort Smith. We can stay out longer and work that way. Sabrina will feed us. I'll get her a camp helper and keep her in wood."

"Sounds good." Andrew scratched his head and squinted. "How many can you brand? I want four thousand."

"Two batches this time, huh?" Jackson shifted his weight to his other leg and chucled. "You're not one to do things small-time, are you, brother?"

"I guess not." If they were going to pull this off, they'd need a banker. The problem would be finding one who would take two kids from the hill country seriously. They had a small record in the Fort Smith deal, and they had some money—but they'd need lots more to ever get them up there.

"Could we do it?"

Andrew stretched and struggled to sit up in the hammock. "I'll just have to put on my boots and go see some big bankers in San Antonio. All they can say is no."

"Then what'll we do?"

He shrugged. "They haven't said no yet."

Jackson shook his head. "Can I start?"

"Sure. I'll need to witch a new well for Sophie first, though. She's afraid ours will run out sometime soon."

"She mentioned it to me."

"After I get that settled, I'll ride over to San Antonio and see some money men. Maybe'll find one who'll take a shot on us."

"How much will it take?"

"A hundred times a hundred."

Jackson punched him in the arm. "Hey, Sophie never taught us how to multiply that high."

"It'll take a lot," Andrew chuckled. "I'll have to set down with her and look at it."

"That's 'tween you and her. Meantime, I'm going to hire some more men and fix the wagon."

"Get to it, brother."

Jackson grinned big. "Oh, yeah—we need more horses, too. We've got about twenty head we don't need to sell, and I'll catch us some more."

"Right on."

"We're going to use some dogs to get them out of the brush. Couple of my boys say they're tough, but they'll bring them out."

Andrew smiled him. "You going to fix that second wagon?"

"I guess I better. We'll need it."

Andrew watched him hurry off. He sighed. Sleep time was over, he guessed. He'd better go talk to Sophie again.

How much would all this cost? A good damn question.

It would not be cheap, though.

Andrew found her resting and drinking coffee at a table.

"Thought you were going to sleep for days." She took a sip. Her eyes still looked puffy from their talk earlier. "I thought you'd be dreaming about your *bruja*."

"Ha-ha." He swung his leg over the bench and joined her. "Sophie, I need to know how much money I'll need to go to Kansas with two large herds."

"Well, that will depend—"

"Jackson's already hiring *vaqueros* to brand them for shipment next spring."

"What's he plan on paying them?"

"I imagine twenty a month."

"Maybe thirty to get experienced ones, huh?"

He frowned. "Maybe, but that might be the bonus if we make money."

She nodded. "We can't do this on a shoestring, kid."

"No, we'll need enough food and supplies to get them to Kansas, just like we did on the trip to Fort Smith. And we'll need about four good horses per man."

She got up to get her tablet and pencils. "How far is it?"

"Eight hundred miles, about."

"Two months plus at fifteen miles a day." She wrote the numbers nearly as fast as he'd said them.

"We won't make that every day. Weather, floods—there'll be days we can't move."

She nodded her understanding. "How many men per herd?"

"Fifteen, plus a cook."

She scribbled it down. "That's six hundred dollars a month for both crews."

"Total time maybe four months, counting gathering and all that, plus part of the coming-home pay."

"And you'll need things like rolls of rope, flour, frijoles, lard, baking powder, bacon, dry apples, raisins, canned peaches, canned tomatoes, rawhide, extra saddles, pads, blankets, canvas—"

"You're getting them down. Nails, hammers, saws, ropes, spices, salt, pepper, sugar...."

"My heavens." She clicked her tongue and shook her head. "Andrew, this is going to be huge."

"Trace chains, harness, an A-frame to hang beef on where there are no trees."

She was silent for a long moment. "What will the cattle bring?"

"More than forty bucks a head, I hope."

"At forty a head, that's eighty thousand dollars." She looked back at him, her eyes wide. "That's *real* money, kid."

"It'll be really big business if we can make it up there with all of them."

"If you can do it, what will you buy?"

"More of Texas. We'd have us lots of land and no one could tell us what to do."

Her eyes were shiny. "I told you that you boys would be big-time ranchers. The pride of Texas. It's coming true."

"The bankers may tell me no, Sophie."

"Do you think they're a bunch of fools?" She tapped the tablet with her finger. "This is big money. That's what they're all about. And you've got a proven business record."

"I guess we'll find out, won't we?" He took a deep breath. "In the meantime, though, I'm going to ask Tasha to come out and find you another well. Jackson and I dug that one with a winch and buckets. I'm not going to do that again."

The next day, with Phil in tow, he rode his new gray gelding back south to the Miguel place. The horse acted excited at first, but soon settled down.

Phil couldn't help but chuckle. "I've never seen you all dressed up like this. You're actually wearing boots! *El patrón* has arrived!"

Tasha's father, Eliza Miguel, met them coming from his corrals and invited them to lunch. Andrew accepted and told him his mission for coming... besides the invitation from Tasha, that is.

"I am sure Tasha would be happy to help find a well for your new *hacienda*. Let's go eat. There is plenty of food."

They thanked him for his hospitality and followed him to the house. Soon they found themselves in a large, tiled dining room being served by pretty girls. Tasha and her mother, Eliza's wife, Rena, joined them.

Eliza began passing out bowls. "Of course, you both remember Philippé. And this is his *patrón*, Mister Andrew Franks."

Across the table, Tasha smiled and nodded at him.

"I think he needs your help Tasha."

She looked surprised. "Mine?"

"He needs a well spotted at his ranch. The *vaqueros* that work for him told him you are the best one to find it."

"Oh, they don't know." She looked down at her hands. "I've missed several."

"Don't worry." Her father smiled at Andrew. "She's being far too humble. She is very good."

"*Papi....*"

He smiled her concern away. "She'll get you a good one."

After the meal, they made plans for her to come to Turkey Track. She could come in three days. That would be Friday, and would stay overnight, with her mother along as a chaperone.

Andrew assured them of decent accomodations. "Sophie has a small house you two can stay in. We're building a much larger house, but it's only about half done right now."

She laughed. "We are not that fancy."

"I'll be looking for you on Friday."

"Oh, we will be there."

"Thanks. I'll owe you a favor if you won't take money."

"No money." Her dark eyes glittered. "But I will find something you can do for me."

Andrew thanked Eliza and Rena for the meal, then took his leave. Tasha fell in beside him on the walk to the stables.

Just like before, she got straight to the point. "Is there a woman in your life?"

He pulled at his shirt collar. "No, I have no one."

"There's a ball in San Antonio. I would like to attend. Can you dance?"

"How much time do I have to learn how?"

She laughed. "You would do that?"

"My cousin Sophie can teach me how. When is it?"

"Next fall. This year's has already passed."

"I will dance by then."

"I will let you know when. Thank you, Andrew."

He took the reins from Philippé and turned to her. If Sophie could make him a businessman, she could make him a dancer. "Thank *you*, Tasha. See you Friday."

"I look forward to it. Ride careful."

And they left her.

Philippé started teasing him as soon as they were out of earshot. "All you need now is to learn how to dance, *patrón*."

A few miles out from the Miguel place, as they were crossing a wide uninhabited stretch of ground, Andrew noticed a cloud of dust rising above the cedars off to their left.

"What's making that dust?" It could be mustangs or even wild cattle on the run, but for some reason, he didn't think so.

"I see it, too. I don't know. "

"You think it might be the Comanches?"

"It damn sure could be."

Andrew jerked the Spencer out of his scabbard and levered in a round.

Phil followed suit with his Winchester. "Where's the best spot to deal with them, do you think? "

"On that rise north of us." He tossed his head at the higher ground. "Make them come at us uphill."

"You're the *patrón.*"

They busted their mounts for the rise and dismounted, hobbling their horses behind them in the cedars.

Andrew heard their war cries first. "I think we got here just in time, Phil."

"They're yacking to get up their nerves."

"Hell, yes, they are. Make your shots count, Phil. They'll be charging hard at us."

A band of war-painted bucks busted out of the brush and into the open ground in front of them. Andrew threw the Spencer to his shoulder and fired. His first bullet took the black-faced leader off his horse and sent him tumbling to the ground.

Beside him, Phil used the Winchester to lead the next brave in line and shot his horse out from under him.

Andrew's next shot nailed another brave, and they hadn't even gotten in arrow range yet. Shocked by their losses, the remaining Comanche veered off into the brush and ducked out of sight to regroup.

Phil thrust his fist into the air. "We won!"

"That's just a start, I figure." Andrew jacked in another round. "They've probably been raiding down in this area and were sneaking back home. I hope they don't want much more war."

"Not yet." The Comanches appeared again, whooping and hollering. Phil stood to aim his rifle. His Winchester spoke and another Comanche went flying off his horse.

Out of the scrum, a loud screaming buck thundered toward them. Andrew's next .50-caliber bullet struck his war-painted chest, swept him off the horse, and silenced him.

And that was it.

The war party went back into the brush to avoid any more shots. In a short time, dust rose above the area where they were and they were soon going northwest. The danger built up drained out of Andrew's face, making his cheeks feel empty.

"We're damn lucky."

"Thank the Virgin Mary, too."

The Comanche didn't want to lose any more men. Two men were not worth dying over. They'd gone for home.

They mounted back up and wasted no time heading home. Andrew felt much better.

They rode into the dooryard long after dark. Too tired to do much more than drop in bed, Andrew slid off the horse to the ground. Sophie, was there, as always, dressed in her robe. She helped him to his feet and walked him to his hammock.

"Tasha's coming Friday. I promised her I'd learn how to dance. Next fall I have to take her to a ball in San Antonio for doing it."

"Sleep tight, big rancher. It'll all still be here for you in the morning. The Pride of Texas." She tucked him in and gave him a kiss on the cheek. "I love you, kid."

FOURTEEN

SOPHIE HAD ORDERED him to buy two new white shirts. He bought them at Maine's General Store in Mason. The owner, a little man in glasses named Neal Maine, fussed over him like some kind of bigwig, sending helpers off to fetch things he needed.

"Word is you're going to Kansas next year."

Andrew stretched his neck against the shirt's stiff collar. "Neal, we're looking hard at it. I'm getting these shirts to wear next week when I go to see the banker in San Antonio about loaning me the money."

Maine looked around to be sure they were alone. "Do you have an amount in mind that you'll need?"

"We've been over it several times and it looks like fifteen thousand dollars, plus all our money."

He nodded. "If you can't borrow it, come back and talk to Arnold and me. We might could help you. I can promise you the best price on everything you need."

"That's lots of money."

"Yes, but you've sold cattle for us and it helped everyone. It settled people's bills we thought we would have to write off."

"I'll give you a chance to bid on it."

Maine's face melted into a smile. "No matter who you do business with in Kansas, just don't bring that much money home on you. Wells Fargo will insure you to get it all into a San Antonio Bank at no risk."

"I'll do that, thank you, sir. I worried about that all the way home from Fort Smith—carrying that much money in coins."

Neal carefully inspected the fit of the shirt, then, gave a nod of approval. "You look very businesslike for a man your age."

"I don't need to tell you, Mr. Maine, I am very serious about this business."

"You can convince them. Or talk to us." They shook hands and Andrew settled the bill. Riding home, he found himself intrigued by the storekeeper's offer. They'd known one another for a while now, and if he were being honest, he'd be far more comfortable working with the people from Mason than some bankers in San Antonio. Whatever happened, though, he was convinced now there would be a way to put these cattle drives on the road.

Tasha and her mother arrived at the ranch before lunch the next day. Sophie and Andrew welcomed them in the dooryard, before Sophie ushered them into the house to their room. Rena told them to go ahead and start work immediately, if they felt like it, while she rested in the house.

They met outside again after Tasha had changed. She now wore a wide-brimmed hat and some kind of gray romper. She held a forked stick in both hands and took measured steps along the northern side of the new *hacienda*. As she walked, she looked suspended in emotionless repose.

Nothing happened.

They made another pass, this time on the west side. She stopped and told a ranch hand to place a flag there. Ten steps further on, she had him place another one.

"I think these two spots are your best chance to get water."

Sophie thanked her and suggested they go to the cook shack. Sabrina had lunch ready, and had rounded up Tasha's mother to be there. He joined them for their meal, and the women talked openly.

Sophie took a bite and wiped her mouth with her handkerchief. "We only have one well and windmill. I worry it might run out with all the activity we have going on here now."

Tasha looked back to Andrew. "And that's your new house?"

"That's Sophie's project. She hired some more workers recently so it would be done someday soon."

Tasha laughed. "And I have never met your twin."

He waved it away. "Jackson should be here this evening. He's really getting busy setting up branding crews."

"They say you look very much alike."

"Oh, they do." Sophie reached over and tousled his hair affectionately. "But I can tell them apart."

"How long have you been here?"

"We've lived on this place about four years." He forked another bite into his mouth. "We settled first in Mason, but our father moved us up here after two years down there."

"Was he a dreamer?"

"Pa?" The question surprised him. "No, he was all business. Didn't spend any money."

"I guess he didn't have any."

What was she getting at? "That was in his plan, too, I'm sure."

"I've heard the story about what happened to him and your mother. I am so sorry for you and Jackson."

He shrugged, vaguely uncomfortable. "It was bad, but we had to take charge and get things going. Sophie came to help us and she's really been a big partner."

"What will you do next?"

"Get two herds together and take them to Kansas."

"Oh my, that would be serious."

He shook his head, feeling impressed that she was interested in his future plans. But didn't she understand that he'd already made one big drive with those cattle, and it had worked out well? Oh, she'd heard people talk about the money he'd made for them. But maybe it wasn't a big enough deal to her—like him going to Abilene was going to be real dangerous compared to the last trip.

"And you—I mean Sophie—are building a large house here?"

"She's part of us. The large house is for all of us."

She frowned at him as they stood outside the small main house in the afternoon's hot wind. "Oh, I thought—"

He smiled. "Let me tell you about our cousin." Then he told her the story about Judge Watkins requiring them to have a guardian, their run-in with Jack McCory, and how Sophie had helped settle things in their life.

When he finished his story, she nodded. "I see. Yes, she should be part of this ranch. Your building her this big house will be nice for her."

They saddled two horses and he gave her a tour of the ranch. He showed her some of the water boxes they'd built that worked in the intermittent streams to draw water for stock during the dry times. It was something Pa had seen work someplace he'd been and they'd busted their butts getting them installed under his orders.

Like so many of Pa's projects, he and Jackson had hated them, but had grown up enough now to see how much they helped keep range cattle and horses grazing in the ranch area.

"You mean you built the first one before he started on the pole house?"

"Oh, Tasha, he was a strange man. If he ever got something in his head, you were going to do it right then or die trying."

They walked up the hill to view some more country, and somewhere along the way, her hand slipped in his. He felt guilty at the touch in the calloused circle of his own tough palm. Her fingers felt like flower stems in his grasp. When they reached the summit, the sun was sinking below the western horizon, burnishing the heavens in brilliant hues of red and copper and pink.

"Thank you." She squeezed his hand. "For taking me into your life and sharing it with me today. I am used to talking to boys my own age about petty things like a new horse or an event I don't dare miss. Talking to you is not the same, Andrew Franks. You're more like a man than anyone your own age. You will be a cattle baron. You and your brother. I don't know if it came from your stoic father, or if you were born with big dreams. I am so grateful you brought me here and let me see what you see from this high point. The empire you will have here someday."

Andrew felt cold standing there in the hot, bloody wind. Her words about made him shudder under his sweaty long-sleeved work shirt.

"We better get back or your mother will be upset."

She shook her head. "My mother thinks you are the nicest man-boy in this world."

"Oh, she don't even know me."

"Yes, she is a very strong when it comes to knowing people. The day you came by the ranch to ask for my help, she said so."

"Well let's go back, Sophie will have supper and she'll chew me out for keeping you away all afternoon."

She reached out, took his hand, and they walked slow back to the horses.

FIFTEEN

EARLY MONDAY, DRESSED for town, Andrew rode into San Antonio. It was past eleven o'clock at night when he dismounted at Healey's Stables near the Alamo. He ordered his horse rubbed down and grained, then took his war bag and walked two blocks to the San Antonio Hotel. The desk clerk gave him a key for the third floor and he climbed in bed for a few hours of sleep.

The next morning, he rose, brushed his hair that Sophie had cut two nights before, splashed his face with water from the pitcher and bowl, then dried it. Still hung over from the long ride, he went downstairs and sat on the patio under the mesquite trees and ordered oatmeal and coffee for breakfast. The stiff waiter thanked him and left him to fill his order.

There he sat in the cool morning air, not even knowing what the meal would cost him. This day would be a challenge to match anything he'd ever known. He had to be strong enough so the bankers would be convinced he was their man to loan money to for the drive. Two herds going up to Kansas for the price of one.

Emanuel Sticks at the Southwest Bank leaned back in his big leather chair and said his bank was uncertain about the future of so-called cattle markets in Kansas. Tenting his fingers in a nervous way, the man continued to lecture him on the pitfalls of cattle drives and the losses that his bank had taken the past season with drovers. Even the presentation he'd brought along—the one Sophie had written in her best penmanship—showing their profits on the Fort Smith trip failed to impress the man. "You realize feeding corn to those animals on the road was a risky business?"

Andrew sighed, coming close to the end of his patience. "No, Mister Sticks, I realize I came in the wrong bank this morning. You obviously have no interest in loaning me the money to make this drive, so thanks for your time and trouble."

"Young man, you have just shown me you do not have the needed maturity or patience to make this operation work, anyway."

"Am I supposed to sit here and listen to your advice all day, sir? No thank you. But down the road when my plan works out, just remember we could have done business together. I can find my own way out."

At the Cattleman's Bank, he cooled his heels for the better part of an hour before finally being ushered in to see the Vice President Hiram Stoneman. From behind a desk covered in deeds and business papers, the big, gray-haired man frowned down at him.

"I see that you are Mister Andrew Franks of Los Olivos, Texas?" He'd read it off a card handed to him when the secretary had showed him in. He acted busy with some papers on his desktop. "Have a seat. What do you need, young man?"

"A fifteen-thousand-dollar loan to get two herds of two thousand head to Abilene next spring."

He didn't bother looking up from his paperwork. "I wish you lots of luck finding a banker who would risk that sum on a boy."

"I am not a boy, sir. I am a successful cattle drover and have produced results. Right here." He tried to hand the Fort Smith cattle drive sheet to the man to read.

"Read it to me."

"'Herein let it be known that Andrew Franks of the Turkey Track brand delivered four hundred head herd of prime steers to the Fort Smith Market on September 10th, 1865 for a profit that earned him over $18,000.'" Andrew looked up. "Would you want me to go on?"

The man took off his wire-framed glasses, sat back in his chair, and shook his head. "If you did that, I want you to get me two telegrams. One from your cattle buyer and the bank that issued that check to verify you did that."

"How do you want the telegrams to come to you?"

"To Hiram Stoneman, Vice President, Cattleman's Bank, San Antonio, Texas."

"I can do that, sir."

"Good, make an appointment when I have them. You really drove four hundred head to Fort Smith and sold them for that?"

"Yes sir."

"That's very impressive. Where is Los Olivos?"

Andrew smiled for the first time. "There's damn sure ain't no olive trees out there. It's west of Mason."

"Get me those telegrams and I'll talk business with you."

He left the man laughing and told him he'd see him shortly.

At the telegraph office, he sent John Hazelton, c/o the Fort Smith, Arkansas First Bank Building a telegram explaining what he needed sent to the Cattleman's Bank, then another to the Fort Smith bank requesting they do the same regarding the check he'd been paid with.

They brought the telegram from Hazelton to the hotel later that evening. Both he and the bank had wired Stoneman at the bank all the information, and they wished him good luck.

Andrew celebrated by eating a three-dollar steak for supper at the hotel restaurant. Then he wrote Sophie and Jackson a letter relating the events of the afternoon and that he might just have the loan they needed based on the fall cattle deal. The food, he wrote, was all high-priced and he was ready to come back home.

He mailed it from the hotel and went upstairs to sleep.

Hiram Stoneman had his desk cleared the next morning when the secretary showed him in his office. The banker stood, shook his hand, told him to have a seat.

"Tell me about the Turkey Track Ranch, Andrew."

"We have a deed for three hundred sixty acres. My brother Jackson, our guardian Sophie, and myself operate the ranch. My parents are dead. We've sold horses all year long in Fort Worth."

Stoneman nodded, apparently deep in thought. "Do you have these cattle? I mean own them?"

"I'll have half those cattle gathered by next spring or close to it. Then I'll take small ranchers' cattle in the second drive."

"Are there that many cattle out there?"

"I have several teams of *vaqueros* out there right now rounding them up. We'll have the cattle. That, sir, I promise you."

"How did you hire them?"

"I treat them nice and feed them good."

Stoneman laughed. "I think we can make this loan. How old are you?"

"Seventeen, sir."

"I'd swear you were at least twenty-five. You're a real businessman. I've talked to big successful cattlemen who could not have make a presentation like you did. One thing—send any monies you get up there in Kansas down here with Wells Fargo. I don't know the tough men who have been robbed coming home from Kansas and other places north."

"I heard that from another businessman."

"I'll send you a letter on the terms that you, your brother, and your guardian will all need to come here and sign for the loan."

"What's the interest rate?"

"Ten percent."

"Thank you." He shook Stoneman's hand. "I have a ranch to run. We'll be here whenever you need us."

"God bless you, Andrew Franks. It's been a real pleasure to meet you."

He picked up his war bag from the hotel and checked out, then liberated his horse from the livery and lost no time heading for home. That night, he slept in a farmer's hay shed. The man's wife fed him breakfast and refused his offer to pay her. He set out for the Turkey Track at first light. Late that night, he rode Gray into the ranch.

A light came on in the house. Sophie came out in her robe and offered to feed him. He shook his head and stripped out his latigos.

"You get my note?"

She shook her head. "No."

"They're making us the loan."

She wrapped him up in a hug. "That's wonderful!"

"Your paper sold him."

"I knew you'd get it. You were too fresh-looking not to."

"Oh, my Sophie, I do need some sleep." He dropped his shoulders in surrender. With his promise to be up to join her for breakfast, he headed for the bunkhouse.

All they had left was to capture the needed cattle.

SIXTEEN

STILL DEAD TIRED, Andrew dressed and went to the cook shack the next morning. No sign of Jackson. He must be out with his *vaqueros*. Good, he hoped they were making big catches.

Sophie had a well report waiting for him. They'd gone down ten feet and hit rock.

"In the old well we got through that layer. It isn't thick," he assured her as she served him eggs, ham, and biscuits.

"They are drilling to blast it today."

"I wish them luck."

She managed to keep a straight face. "Maybe you could go down and see about it."

"Boy, I hated that well-digging business. No. Hell, no." He scooped a forkful of eggs into his mouth. "I wouldn't be any help, anyway. Jackson and I were little kids when we dug that old well, maybe twelve years old. I was half as tall as I am now."

"He had twelve-year-old boys down there doing that?"

"Who in the hell else did he have but us two to do it?"

She laughed. "Tell me about San Antonio."

"I went first to see this banker who just wanted to lecture me on what I should do."

"What did he tell you?"

"I don't know. I stopped listening to him at a certain point. I got up and told him so."

She shook her head, obviously amazed that anyone had the guts to do that to a banker. "What next?"

"Then I went to Cattleman's. This Stoneman had a big mess on his desk and was about as interested in me at first as if I was a fly buzzing around his head."

"What did you do?"

"I read our report on what happened in Fort Smith. He stopped me and told me that if I got proof from that bank and the cattle buyer that I'd made the business—that if they sent him telegrams with the details—he'd consider a loan. Old Hazelton got right on it up there at Fort Smith, and so did the bank. I went in the next day and we talked about the Turkey Track and the three of us. He could hardly believe we'd done that sale and said my plan beat most big cattleman that came in for those kinds of loans."

She jumped up and hugged his head. "By God, you two *will* be big cattlemen someday, I swear."

He laughed at her enthusiasm and stood up to hug her tight. "We'll manage to do that with your help—somehow."

She swept her hair back from her face. "Lordy, I came out here on a mission, and ends up we are really doing something."

"I also had a talk with Mister Maine over in Mason when I bought those white shirts. He told me they'd finance the drive if we couldn't get money down there. He asked for our business and promised to have the lowest prices for our needs."

"That was sure nice of him."

"I thought so, too. So people are taking us serious." He wiped his mouth with his napkin and carried his plate over to the counter.

"Where you going?"

"To spread some of this on Jackson."

"Good. He's working hard out there."

"I know. He's grown up a lot, too."

"Amen to that."

He turned and leaned against the counter, crossing his arms. "You haven't seen any sign of McCory, have you?"

"No. Maybe he died."

Andrew laughed. "No such luck."

"Hey, where's Phil? He's supposed to be riding with you."

"Out helping Jackson."

She gave him what he thought of as "the mom look." "Put him in your back pocket and take him with you. We've talked about this before, Andrew."

"Yes, ma'am."

"No, take him along with you." She hung on the cook shack doorframe to scold him again.

He left the ranch and headed west on the stout red roan horse, Strawberry, short-loping him most of the way. This was one of the mustangs they'd rounded up, only to discover he was likely an escaped Comanche war pony. After riding him some, Jackson had them put in the using-horse pen. Andrew liked his gaits and power.

He reached the first chuckwagon and Sabrina, wearing a fresh apron, waved him over.

"You've got here just in time to eat, *patrón*. I can get you a big hunk of fire-broiled beef to gnaw on. I've been cooking them slow over some mesquite all afternoon."

He laughed. "You're a dandy. I'll be glad to test it for you. How are things going?"

"They've been working real hard. Very long days, but they're getting lots of cattle branded."

"Good. Are you getting along here?"

"I love these *vaqueros*. This is the best job I have ever had.

This wagon is so nice and I have tent of my own. Thank you so much for everything."

"You need something, you complain."

Jackson and his weary crew drug in close to sundown. Andrew could see immediately that his hard-charging brother was working them too hard. If he didn't give them a break they'd quit him.

"See you made it." Breathing hard, Jackson pulled off his gloves and dropped down on a bench. "How're things at the ranch?"

"Fine. Our loan's been approved. Let me tell you, though, Jackson—these men need a break. And so do you."

Jackson's face darkened. "We're just working cattle. I've got close to three hundred head branded. What's the problem."

"Damn it, Pryor. They need a break."

Jackson blinked at him in disbelief. "*Pryor?*"

"You're acting exactly like him. We need to pay them a few dollars and let them go down to San Juan. Get drunk, find some women, relax for a couple of days."

He sighed, let his head fall back against the bench. "I suppose you're right. Dammit, I guess I have my mind so set to match you getting us that loan, I wanted to get them all branded."

"Nothing wrong with that."

"We've been working hard. Guess we can get some money from Sophie for some time off?"

"I'll ride back tonight and bring the money up here so they have a few dollars each to spend on raising hell."

"Be sure to take Phil along." Jackson's tone was stern. "You and I could always help each other. I worry about you out on the road alone."

"Yeah, yeah. Sophie said the same damn thing." Andrew waved him way and looked out to the horizon. "You best eat some supper. Sabrina's done good today."

"She's great. You couldn't beat her. She has suppliers bring her good things to fix."

They walked to the line of men ready to eat

Jackson stuck his fingers in his mouth and whistled. "Hey, listen up, the *patrón* is here. He wants us to rest a few days in San Juan. I'm sending him home to get us a few dollars for us to spend."

The men in line threw their *sombreros* in the air and shouted. Dust flew as they clapped each other on the back in celebration.

Jackson gave him a nod. "That'll work."

"I'll be back tomorrow."

"Wait. Take Phil with you."

"He's been working all day—"

"He'll want to go with you. Let him eat."

"All right." He borrowed a cup from Sabrina's stock and poured himself a cup of coffee. It meant a lot to him that everyone was so concerned for his safety, but it seemed like a lot of inconvenience.

He found Phil sitting just outside the circle of the fire, eating his dinner quietly. "Hey, partner."

"Hey, *patrón*. You—didn't bring any oatmeal, did you?"

Andrew shot him a smirk. "Nah. You got lucky tonight. Jackson says you need to ride with me back to the ranch."

His mouth full, the other man nodded in agreement and swallowed hard. "I'll get a fresh horse."

"Eat first." He restrained him with a grip on his shoulder. "We have all night."

Their ride home was star-studded. It was past midnight when they got back, and Sophie lighted a lamp at the sound of them putting up their horses.

She came out in her robe. "Anything wrong?"

"Nah, Jackson's crew just needs a break. I came to get them a little money so they can let off some steam."

"We can do that." She held up her lantern. "Hey, Phil. You doing all right this evening?"

"Hi, Sophie. I'm doing fine. Jackson just thought he needed a shadow."

"He does, by God. *All* the time. Stop letting him slip away without you, you hear me?"

Phil removed his hat and bowed deeply. "I live only to serve you, *señorita.*"

"Well." Sophie's face colored in the light of the lamp, and she self-consciously readjusted her robe around her. "If nothing else, you've sure got one hell of a silver tongue, boy. Hope you shoot as well as you talk."

"Humility forbids me from answering, *señorita.*"

Andrew had managed to hold back his laughter up until then, but *that* did it. Shoulders shaking, he lost control, laughing so hard tears started rolling down his face.

"Damn kids." Sophie rolled her eyes and turned back toward the house. "I'll see you at breakfast."

He wiped his eyes. "We'll be there."

Awake at dawn, they dressed and joined her at the cook shack. Out by the new house, Sophie had three hands digging the well beside her expanded building crew.

Standing in the doorway drinking coffee, Andrew yawned as he watched them digging. "They found any moisture down there yet?"

Sophie shook her head. "Nope. When you boys dug the other one, did the water run in fast?"

"Yeah. I didn't think Pa was gonna let us out before we both got drowned."

"I warned them. Jackson said the same thing." She was serving them scrambled eggs, pancakes, and fried bacon. Phil brought the coffee pot and refilled everyone's cup.

She put a leather pouch on the table. "There's eighty dollars in here. Bring back what's left."

"Yes, ma'am."

"Listen to him." She looked at Philippé and pulled the hair back from her face again. "He acts like I'm his boss."

"You *are* my boss." Andrew shook his head as Phil laughed. "Nobody else orders me around."

"Well speaking of the boss, we'll need a builder to roof our new house soon, *patrón*."

"Not you, too." He shook his head in mock disgust. "Okay, okay. I'll see what there is at San Juan."

"Thank you."

After breakfast, he and Phil rode back to the cow camp. The men came in early that evening and Jackson paid each man five dollars as an advance. That left five dollars in his bag when he was through, and Andrew told him to pocket it.

Plans were for them to be off Friday and Saturday and come back Sunday afternoon. Monday, they'd go back to work. Everyone agreed. Five of the men were going home to their wives. That left ten to celebrate in the village.

The horse wrangler, a young boy they all called Boots, was to keep the horses grazing and getting them rested. Sabrina and her helper were going to watch the camp.

Andrew and Jackson discussed the situation with Phil over dinner. Andrew thought they should trail along, so the men had no trouble. It was a quiet place, but one never knew when hell could break loose. When they left the table to saddle up, Andrew recalled his pa and the *cantina* girl affair again. He wondered what a woman and a situation like that was like. He was sure he'd learn someday.

San Juan planned a fiesta when their outfit arrived. Andrew tried some homemade beer—his first—and didn't like it. He shoved his glass over to one of the *vaqueros*.

"Bad stuff."

The man took a big gulp of it. "Oh, *patrón*, that isn't so bad. I've drank some real bad stuff. Lots worse than this."

"You can have it." Andrew stood up to leave the sour, nicotine-smelling place. He'd have to find something else to do. This was just not his place.

Phil joined him out on the porch.

"I think I need a nap."

His friend and bodyguard scanned the village around them. "Where can you do that?"

"At the stables, maybe. Bet I could flake out in some hay."

"I bet you can."

"You go ahead, this is your time off."

"No problem." Phil gave him a head toss to go on.

Situated in a haystack in the livery, Andrew took off his gun belt, wrapped it around the holster, laid down on a blanket, and nodded to Phil. A little sleep wouldn't hurt him.

He woke to the sound of something clacking. His first sight was a near-naked woman wearing veils dancing in the bloody light of sundown in the barn alleyway. Sitting cross-legged nearby, Phil was watching her every cat-like move. She had the beat in her fingers with those castanets, and she kept saying *olé*.

Andrew rolled over and went back to sleep.

It was dark when Phil woke him again. The same woman was there, only now in a blouse and skirt.

Phil gestured to her. "This is Anita. She wants us to go eat with her now."

Andrew could leave the rest to his imagination. With her arms wrapped around both men's waists, and a broad smile on her face, she led them to the town square, where the people of the village had half a steer cooking on a large spit. Music was playing, and folks were dancing in the dust. Everyone from the surrounding area must have come to the village to celebrate with them.

The woman talked endlessly, pointing out all the things there were to eat. Then when he didn't move fast enough for her satisfaction, she fixed him a blanket-size tortilla wrapped around a mixture of beef, fried peppers, onions, and *frijoles*. She led him around the square introducing him to everyone like some kind of auctioneer. He nodded, shook hands, tried to find a kind word or

two to say to everyone, and wondered if there was anyone here
he could find with the skills to finish Sophie's house.

They finally found a bench to eat on. The red wine Anita
served him with his meal was much better than the beer from
earlier. He'd had time to decide she was probably in her twenties.
She had large breasts and kept pushing them into both him and
Phil whenever she had the chance. What was her purpose? Had
she found Phil, or had he found her?

No telling.

After the meal, she made him get up and dance with her.
Andrew considered himself three-footed, but she soon had him
dancing some kind of jig, with her in his arms pressed close against
him. Holding her and moving to the music under the paper
lanterns, he felt more than just a little self-conscious and nervous.

She stood on her toes to whisper in his ear. "Have you ever
loved a woman?"

He shook his head.

"Tonight, we will do that."

His heart stopped.

Would lightning strike him dead if he did such a thing? All
Pa's warnings. Those hellfire sermons they'd attended in Arkansas
at those revival camp meetings.

Had the devil sent her to snare him?

The touch of her hand on his back straightened him up.
"Smile, *mia amigo*. You will like it. I promise."

They danced. He'd see how he liked it. Time would tell,
and meanwhile, he could think of all the things that could go
wrong for him doing this. Where was Jackson when he needed
his advice?

Hell, his brother probably knew less than he did about what
lay ahead for him. Damn….

SEVENTEEN

BIRDS WERE SINGING. A rooster crowed out in the yard, and some goats cried to be milked somewhere nearby. Andrew opened his matted eyelashes, finding himself alone on a pallet in the cool morning air. He'd not slept alone the night before.

Where was Anita?

Stumbling around the room, he snatched up his clothes and pulled them on, strapped on his holster, and poked his head out the door.

He found her cooking outside. She looked up at him with a broad, knowing smile. "Sleep well?"

"Yes." He nodded dumbly. "Thanks for your kindness."

"Oh, I was richly rewarded for it. I'm making you a tortilla wrap to take with you for breakfast. Philippé came by and said you were needed and I was to wake you. Here." She handed him the food.

"Did Phil say something was wrong?"

"He said nothing, only that he needed to find your brother. Eat. He plans to come back. Your roan is saddled." She turned up her palms and moved in to kiss him. "Thank you for making a widow's evening so fine."

He let the kiss linger for a time, then pulled away. "I owe you."

"No." She shook her head to dismiss his concern. "I hope you can solve whatever this matter is quickly and come back to see me again."

Horses were coming. He hugged her one last time, then ran for his roan at the corral.

Jackson looked more than a little worse for wear. "Our little horse wrangler Boots came by an hour ago and found Phil. Someone's stolen all our ranch horses at the cow camp."

Andrew hopped up into the saddle. "We can catch them."

Jackson looked hard at him, reined his horse around, then spoke to Anita like he knew her. "Good sumbitch, wasn't he?"

She beamed proudly. "You promised me he would be one."

Jackson grinned like a mouse-catching cat. So that was it. It had all been a damn setup from the very beginning—a planned seduction. Rascals—Phil and Jackson and Lord knew who else had been in on it. Who else? He'd find them, by God—every last one—and get even with them somehow.

Red-faced, Andrew twirled a finger in the air over his head. "Daylight's burning boys. Let's ride."

They left the village in a cloud of dust.

He waved at Jackson to get his attention. "Is Sabrina alright?"

His brother, still looking smug over the trick they'd managed to pull on him, nodded. "Boots said there were four of them. They rode into shooting like they knew we had nobody there watching over the place. Our people took cover, and the rustlers rounded up all the horses and drove them north."

"North?" No damn border bandits would head that way.

"Yeah. He said north."

"Nevermind, we'll get them."

They picked up the rustler's trail a couple of miles north of the cow camp. From the tracks, it was clear the thieves were moving the herd fast. How did they expect to escape? There was no way for them to get away with a hundred horses. Did the rustlers expect them to just forget about their livestock? Like hell. That was his *remuda* and it would be costly to replace them—no, they were going to catch these damn bandits and hang them for it.

He pushed the roan harder. After four hours or so of hard pursuit, though, he realized it would be a longer chase than he'd originally thought. They'd need to find some food and a place to stop and rest the horses. When he held up his hand to walk their lathered horses, Jackson rode up beside him.

"We need to find some food, Andrew. This chase is going to take longer than we thought."

"I just had the same thought." He took off his hat and wiped the sweat from his forehead with the sleeve of his shirt. "We can go to Dry Creek. We can buy some food there. It's only a few miles east at the next crossroad.

"Sounds like a plan."

"I wish I knew those bastards' names."

"Why? We catch them they won't be around long."

Jackson nodded. "Makes me furious they'd steal our horses."

Andrew laughed. "Brother, did you ever think the three of us are the rich ones around here?"

"Hell, we ain't that rich."

"Compared to what? We are compared to all of our Mexican rancher neighbors. Richer than a lot of the white trash trying to build ranches out here."

"I guess you're right." His brother shrugged and looked off into the distance. "But two pair of pants ain't rich in my book."

"Remember when we couldn't pay for a wagonload of corn?"

Jackson reined his hard-breathing horse down some more. "I wondered a lot if we spent all of his loot."

"We may never know." They cantered down the wagon tracks leading off to Dry Creek. "Hey, Phil, what do you think about these thieves?"

"They were bold enough. I don't know what they think they can do with that many horses, though."

"Me, either. But they must have a plan."

The *vaquero* bodyguard booted his bay gelding up beside them and shook his head. "Thieves are never that smart, though."

They laughed, but Andrew remembered another one of Pa's old saws—there was a first time for everything.

Dry Creek needed some rain, all right. A small, dusty huddle of a few shacks, businesses, and a post office. The saloon was unpainted except for the sign of a star over on the false front. Weathered dark wood and a few hipshot horses at the hitching post made it look even drearier.

They dismounted and went inside.

A bartender in shirtsleeves and garters greeted them with a professional smile. "What's your pleasure gentlemen?"

"We need some food."

"I can get you some food. Beer?'

"We'd take some of that, too."

"I'll get our barmaid to fix it." The man began drawing beer into mugs.

A mustached man seated at a table with a bottle of whiskey and a glass gave them a hard look. "You guys new around her?"

Andrew nodded. "Our *remuda* was stolen. We're on their trail."

"Well, they didn't come though here."

"No, they went north. West of here. We'll catch 'em."

He laughed out loud. "Sure you will. Two boys and a spic."

Before Andrew could stop him, Jackson had stomped across the room and flung the man's table over, spilling him on his back. With his pistol in the man's face, he spoke through his teeth. "We're the gawdamn Franks Brothers and we demand respect from you and anyone else. We're Texas ranchers and we ain't kids or white trash. You savvy?"

"Yeah. Yeah. I's only asking."

Andrew pulled the man to his feet and Phil set the table back up. They set the remains of his bottle and glass on it. "I didn't mean nothing, I promise."

Andrew called over to the bartender to bring the man another beer. "Then don't call us kids and our man a spic. We'll run down those rustlers and settle with them."

"I don't doubt it in the least."

Andrew walked Jackson back over to the bar. The rest of customers gave them a wide berth after that display. His brother had done lots of growing up in the past year, but his temper could still be a problem.

At least nobody like McCory would ever run over or badmouth them again, though.

A Mexican woman brought them some tortilla-wrapped food. He settled the bill and gave her a nice tip. After that, they went back outside and mounted up.

Jackson was silent as they rode out of town. Riding next to him, Andrew frowned and punched him on the arm. "Hey. You okay there, partner?"

"I guess I just lost it back there," he said after a moment. "But he made me blind mad calling us boys and Phil a spic. Sumbitch'll know better next time."

"I just don't want you to pick a fight you can't win, Jackson. Phil and I had your back, though. We damn sure ain't boys any longer. I figure we been men since we laid Pa in his grave."

The next morning before dawn, Andrew woke with his eyelashes glued with trail dust. He would have given almost anything to to sleep a little longer, but knew that would be impossible. If he wanted to be a real rancher, this was part of it. He forced himself into a sitting position, rubbed his eyes, and got up to wake his partners. They had miles to ride that day and rustlers to catch. After some dry jerky for breakfast, they saddled up and rode on.

Late in the day they stopped at a ranch house near the trail. A tall, striking woman with gray in her hair answered the door.

Andrew took off his hat and held it to his chest. "Sorry to bother you, ma'am, but we're chasing horse rustlers and would like to buy a meal."

"I won't sell you a meal, but I'll sure fix you something. You boys wash up and come inside."

"Ma'am, we're, uh— well, to be honest, we're pretty dusty from being in the saddle two days—"

"I'm not blind. My name is Lou. This is my house. Please, come inside."

"Well, thanks. I'm Andrew Franks." He gestured back to his companions, both still mounted. "That's my brother Jackson, and our partner, Philippé—thought we just call him Phil."

"Nice to meet you. Wash up and come in."

"Yes, ma'am."

She stuck her head back out the door. "And call me Lou. I ain't no ma'am."

"Yes—ah, *Lou*."

Jackson laughed. "She's our kind of folks.

While sitting down waiting for supper, they learned that Lou's husband, Earle, was out checking on their cattle. When she found out all they'd eaten was jerky during the day, she about had a fit to make Sophie proud. Andrew explained the importance of catching those thieves with two cattle drives facing them in the coming season.

"You young men ever drove a herd before?" She busied herself making biscuit dough.

"We sure have." Jackson poured himself another cup of coffee. "We've took four hundred head to Fort Smith last winter and fed them corn most of the way. They were fat as hogs and we topped the market."

"How do you feed four hundred steers corn?"

Jackson laughed. "With a scoop shovel out of a wagon. Andrew promised the man fat cattle, and we gave him what he asked for."

"You don't have parents?"

"No." Andrew shook his head. "They died last year. Our cousin Sophie came down from Arkansas to be our guardian."

"She must be a great lady."

He couldn't argue with that. "She's all that and more. And a real partner in our business, too."

"I know you boys want to get on, but cooking takes time."

Jackson turned suddenly serious, and placed both his palms down on the table. "Lou, we'd wait half a day for your cooking and ride hard afterwards."

She laughed. "You haven't even tasted it yet."

"It'll beat dry jerky, believe me." Jackson raised his cup for a sip and shook his head. "We usually come more put-together than this, but we thought we could catch them by now."

"How many are there?"

"We aren't certain." Deep in thought, Andrew rubbed a thumb on the tabletop. "We only had a lady camp cook and two young wranglers in camp when they raided them."

"I see."

"We're gonna catch them and get our damn horses back."

Her blue eyes twinkled. "You know, I believe you will"

Or die trying.

EIGHTEEN

TWO DAYS LATER, just across the Brazos River and still headed north, Jackson's horse went lame. That forced them to stop and buy a horse from a rancher they found nearby. He had three horses he offered to sell, a dun with a crooked front leg that didn't bother his gaits, a long-neck bay, and a stout, roman-nosed sorrel that probably hadn't been gelded till he was five or six.

Jackson chose the roman-nosed sorrel and Andrew paid the man twenty bucks. Robbery, for sure, but they didn't have all day to dicker. Jackson immediately took to calling the new mount Spook, after he went sideways up the dusty road headed north single-footing—but he'd get over that. Andrew just shook his head, amused at his brother's choice of mounts. It was his horse and he acted like he could single-foot all day. For him, he wanted no part of a horse like that to ride hour after hour.

The rancher mentioned having seen the dust from the herd the day before and wondering about it. If Jackson's horse hadn't gone lame, they might have caught them already, judging from what the man told them.

Hopefully, though, by this time they no longer worried about anyone chasing them.

Philippé sat in his saddle and studied the recent horse apples in the hoof prints on the trail. "We're getting closer."

By sundown, they stopped in a small-town saloon, ate a meal, and made camp on a small creek just outside of the village.

Sitting by the fire, Jackson cut off another bite of jerky from a hunk and popped it in his mouth. "Tomorrow's the day we catch them, boys. Them horses sure must be road weary, the way they've been driving them."

Phil nodded. "I bet they're riding fresh mounts every day, too."

"I guess they could. They've sure got enough."

At dawn, they ate some pastries Andrew had bought the night before from a Danish housewife whose house they'd passed on the road. Saddling up, they rode north again, through a small valley and up over the rise beyond....

...and there in the great cradle of huge, grassy prairie was their horse herd.

He got out his brass telescope and looked them over. He saw many he recognized or had ridden in previous months. Then he scanned about for the rustlers. After a few moments, he found them, too—or at least smoke from their cookfire. They must have gotten a late start this morning and were just now preparing their breakfast.

Without a word, Andrew reached and drew the Spencer from its scabbard. Behind him and to either side, Jackson and Phil did the same with their Winchesters. Actions clicked and rounds were chambered.

The time had come.

"Shoot to kill?"

"Yep." Andrew nodded, then turned to look at the other member of their party. Over the past few months, Philippé had become more than a simple bodyguard and employee.

He was family now, too. "You ready, Phil?"

Phil gave him a wicked, wolfish grin. "Say the word, *patrón*."

All right.

"Follow my lead, but don't get too close. That way, they can't take out more than one of us with a lucky shot from a scattergun." Balancing the Spencer across his knees, he pulled his .44 and checked his load. "Watch out for riders on the flanks, too. Boots said there were four of them when they raided the camp, but there could just as easily be more. Got me?"

Nods all around.

He holstered the Colt. "Let's do this, boys."

They took off toward the camp at a dead run, scattering the herd as they went. As they drew closer, the rustlers came into view, sitting around the campfire like Andrew thought.

A big, ugly man in a porkpie hat jumped up the from the log he'd been sitting on, threw down his cup of coffee, and went for his piece. Reining up, Andrew lifted the Spencer to his shoulder, took aim, and fired. The shot took the man straight in the chest and sent him flying ass over backwards in a bloody spray of scarlet. As he fell, another man, this one younger and hatless, lunged behind the same log and raised a shotgun. Andrew swiveled right, jacked in another round, and pulled the trigger. The .50 caliber slug took the other boy square in the face, right between the eyes.

Meanwhile, Jackson and Phil had passed him, veering off left and right after the remaining rustlers. Jackson missed with his first shot, but connected with the second, hitting another cowboy headed for his horse and putting him flat on his face in the dirt.

The last two managed to make it to their horses and actually saddle up. Phil got the first one, shooting the man's horse out from under him and sending him tumbling across the grass.

Jackson was in pursuit of the last rider. He, too, went for the easy shot and went for the horse instead of the rider. Once both were on the ground, he rode over and used his .44 to put them both out of their misery.

Andrew stuck the Spencer in his scabbard, dismounted, and

drew his Colt to check the devastation in the camp. He was only twenty feet away when a man with a bloody shoulder rose ahead of him, pistol drawn. Andrew turned and fired in the same moment the other man pulled the trigger.

The movement saved his life. The rustler's shot went wide to the right, cracking past Andrew's ear like a hot and bloody wind. The other man wasn't so lucky, taking Andrew's .44 ball in the left side of his neck. Rich, red blood gushed from the wound like a fountain, and he fell in a heap where he was.

Another moaning rustler was on his belly, trying to crawl away. Andrew walked over calmly and dispatched him like they did Comanche, with a shot to the back of the head.

Only his boots tried to kick his way into hell, shot hard and face down.

Phil came back. Still mounted, he had another dead rustler dragging along behind him on the end of his lariat. Jackson was close behind with another one. Andrew took a count. With the two injured ones he'd just dispatched, that made six, all dead. And not a familiar face in the bunch for him.

Jackson untied his lariat and started winding it back up. "We burying 'em?"

"Hell no." Andrew holstered his Colt and spat on the last one he'd shot. "Let the buzzards eat the bastards. That's what they get for stealing our horses. I —"

He stopped. He'd just seen movement in the brush just west side of camp. Someone was out there.

"Stand up!" Colt back in hand, he jumped over the remains of the rustler's fire and cocked the hammer back on the run. "Hands up! No tricks!"

Out of the greasewood stood a young white girl, wet-eyed and shaking. She wore only a short slip, exposing dirty legs and brown hair that badly needed combed. She was probably sixteen or seventeen.

"Who are you?

"Uh... C— Callie. Callie Sanders."

"Where you from?"

"Gates."

He'd never heard of it. "What were you doing here?"

"T— they kidnapped me."

He didn't believe a word of it. She was more likely one of the outlaw's concubines. "Go get dressed. We're leaving here shortly."

Jackson took off his hat and scratched his scalp as he watched her coming in. "Who's she?"

"She says her name is Callie. Said she'd been kidnapped."

"You believe her?"

"Hell, no. I'd say she was living with them."

She pulled a dress over her head, wiggling it down over her chest, then her waist. "You two going to kill me like you did them or what?"

Andrew holstered his gun again and sighed. "Make us some food. We're starting back to south Texas when we finish our meal. You can go along or we'll give you a horse and you can ride the other way."

"I have no money. I don't know anyone out here."

"Then cook us some food."

She turned and walked off, grumbling under her breath.

Phil went from body to body, checking the outlaws' pockets for knifes and other loot. He came back with his hat full of Confederate money. Upon later count, they ended up with fifty real dollars and some change.

They also collected seven pistols, two rifles, a shotgun, a pile of saddles and several war bags. The extra saddles would be especially handy to have on their big drive.

"We're gonna need to buy a wagon to haul all this home."

Jackson agreed. "Yes, sir, Pryor. Waste not, want not."

Andrew laughed at his words. "I'll go find one after we eat.

You boys can wrangle the herd while I'm gone. They should be easy. Lots of good grazing here and they're already tired. We'll be ready to leave in the morning."

"Eat before you go looking," Jackson said. "It don't smell bad."

The buzzards had found their upcoming feast already. No doubt, the smell of blood had drawn them. A few big ones had already landed about fifty feet from camp, stalking about and making throaty sounds amongst themselves while building the courage to get closer.

The girl must have had some beans on the fire when they'd arrived, because they were already cooked. Her biscuits were all right, but her apple cobbler was good. The coffee was strong, but sure not Arbuckle's. Andrew decided he'd buy some if he found a store nearby.

"Kin I go with you to south Texas if I cook?"

Jackson pointed a fork at his brother. "Ask Andrew. He's the ramrod around here."

Andrew tipped his hat and chewed thoughtfully. "I guess you can come."

"Thank you!" She jumped up with her arms spread wide.

He stopped her with a look. "We're only hiring a cook."

Disappointed at the rejection, Callie flopped down beside Jackson as if seeking his attention. "Some ramrod, huh?"

"By Gawd he's a good one. You'll see."

After supper, Andrew rode on down the road and found a small ranch with a light wagon and large, roan-colored draft mare to pull it in the shafts. After a bit of haggling with the owner, they settled on a price of fifty dollars. With many thanks, Andrew paid the man, tied his own horse to the back of the wagon, and drove it back to camp after sundown.

After the others' inspection, they agreed he'd done well. With that, they drew straws for who would stay up on guard duty. Phil drew the short straw for first watch, and the others turned in.

At breakfast before dawn, Jackson told him the names of the rustlers, which he'd drawn out of Callie while Andrew had been gone the night before. The leader had been a man named Leonard Simms, and he'd been from East Texas. They'd planned to hole up with the herd in the Indian Territory and sell the horses to drovers going up the trail who'd lost their own.

"She said they were mostly army deserters from the Confederacy. Had no work and Simms told them they'd get rich selling horses up there to those drovers who needed them."

Andrew knew how little money there was to hire anyone to do anything in Texas at the moment. Most of the money in the state was worthless Confederate paper. Economic times were sure to be rough ahead. They were lucky to have gotten their loan.

But that also meant opportunity for them—big bargains on land, livestock, even feed, if they played their cards right.

They loaded everything in the wagon and mounted up. On the last rise, Andrew looked back to see a mass of buzzards circling the field, wondering where to land with so many of their own fighting over scraps on the ground. He turned back to the herd, satisfied they were at last headed home.

Jackson rode the lead and the horses followed him. Andrew and Phil had little trouble keeping the others in the herd on either side, with Callie bringing up the rear in the wagon. They sure weren't like longhorns. No wonder a sorry handful of rustlers had managed to get them so far north.

At one point, Phil waved him down to ask a question. "How close were we to the Indian Territory?"

"Probably two days, I figure. I saw some signs for the Red River ferry—twenty miles."

Phil nodded. "We only lost six head from the herd?"

"That was my count. We were lucky."

"Damn lucky, I'd say."

At midday, they took a break and Callie set up to cook a

meal. The horses spread out in the field around them and grazed. While they were stopped, Jackson took the girl aside and spoke to her about how things worked in their outfit. Andrew figured she'd find her way. He certainly wasn't interested in her, and the less he had to do with her, the better.

Before they mounted up again, he asked Jackson to walk with him for a few minutes for a private word.

"What's up?"

"What if we hire some boys to help you drive the herd? Let Phil and me go on home and get things going on our preparations for the drive." They were wasting daylight, and they had commitments to keep now.

Jackson put his hands on his hips and thought about it. "Sure, but we'll be a week or more getting back. Where are the boys?"

"I bet I can put out word. If we offer to pay them ten bucks and feed them, they'll be here quick."

"Let's do it."

Andrew mounted up and headed for the first town off the track. Before he got there, he met two barefoot boys on horseback along the road.

"Want to make ten bucks?"

"Sure, mister. How?"

"Go home and tell your ma you have a job driving horses down to Mason, Texas. It pays ten bucks, and we'll feed you, too. Get her permission, get a bedroll, and go see my brother. He's just west of here with the horses."

"What's his name?"

"Jackson Franks. I need six more boys. You got any friends who can come along? Can you get them today? These horses are broke and easy to drive. You two get me four more boys, I'll pay you five extra dollars apiece."

The freckle-faced boy on the left clapped his hands together and whooped. "Hell, yes, we'll have them there by sundown."

"Good. Remember. Five extra bucks apiece."

"Yes, sir!" They left on their horses on the run. Andrew smiled after them. He'd need to find somewhere to order some more food and get it delivered to Jackson that afternoon.

Once he got into town, he found the store easily and spoke to the young clerk. "I have camp west of town with my horse herd. I need some supplies sent to them today."

"How far away?"

"Four, five miles."

"How much do you need?"

"A sack of flour, sack of *frijoles*, twenty pounds of bacon, couple buckets of lard. Fifty pounds of sugar, couple cases of tomatoes, raisins, dried apples, and some Arbuckle coffee, if you've got any."

"Will this be cash or credit?"

"Cash."

"I'll personally take it out there myself, sir."

A big man in an apron came in the store in a bloody apron a few minutes later. "I have some fresh beef."

"I'll take a quarter of beef—if it's good."

The man nodded. "Big, fat carcass. Bobby says you had a herd of horses west of here?"

"Some rustlers stole them from our ranch. We recovered them and were hiring some boys to help my brother get them home. We live down near Mason, Texas."

"You work for the man owns this ranch?"

"No sir. My brother and I own and run the Turkey Track Ranch at Los Olivos. Our parents died last year and left it to us."

"Oh."

He stuck out his hand. "I'm Andrew Franks."

"Ira Henshaw. Good to meet you. Not many come in here and talk about paying cash these days. I was just curious."

"Good to meet you, too, Ira. I appreciate your delivering

the groceries. We're shorthanded. I'm hiring boys to help get our herd back home. I found several said they'd get me more."

"I bet you have an army out there when the word gets out."

Andrew laughed and paid the clerk. Henshaw thanked him, and he rode back to camp satisfied they'd soon have help.

When he got back, he let Callie know she had food and help on the way.

Using her hand to shade her view of him, she made a face. "I was about out of food."

"I figure he'll be here with a buckboard in a couple of hours. Figure for supper a dozen more."

"I can do that."

He nodded and turned his horse out to go find Jackson. Then he remembered something else he needed to tell her. "There's a beef quarter coming, too."

"Good. I never had that on the menu before."

"Turkey Track ain't some patch-up outfit."

"I can see that."

"I'll go check with Jackson."

"I'll watch for delivery. I'm excited," She started to turn and spun back. "Oh, Andrew. Thank you."

He touched his hat brim to let her know he'd heard her.

The horses looked settled and calm as he walked his own mount through them. This would be an easy drive for Jackson, even with a bunch of greenhorns helping out.

Jackson grinned when he heard the news. "You think of everything, I swear. Thanks, brother."

"I'm going to head for home tonight and get things going. Who's running your branding crew now?"

"Obregon. He's a good one. He should be working hard."

"I hate to leave you with a bunch of tenderfoot boys. You want to keep Phil around? Just in case?"

"Hell, no. You take him along. I'll be fine." He grinned.

"Besides, I don't need Sophie chewing my ass when she finds out he's guarding my back instead of yours."

"She sure would, wouldn't she?" Andrew chuckled and shook his head. God love her. "All right. Those boys'll get out here before sundown. We'll pick and choose the best ones."

"It's all gonna to work out, brother. It'll work fine, and once we can get those cattle up to Kansas, the Turkey Track'll finally be a real ranch."

"When I said I'd pay cash for our supplies the man owned the store came in and shook my hand."

"You done it, Andrew. You done it. I thought that Fort Smith drive was crazy, you made me believe, and you made it happen."

"Not without you."

Jackson slapped him on the back. "Pride of Texas, brother."

"Pride of Texas."

Help arrived before sundown, over a dozen fresh-faced boys anxious for a cash job mounted on horses, ponies, and burros. Andrew took down their names on the back of an old calendar he'd taken from the rustlers, then ordered them to run their horse or pony down to a small tree, round it, and race back. He judged each one's ride and control of their horse by what a rider would need if the mustangs spooked. He soon had his list of the ones who he thought had made the cut. Once they'd all made their run, he gathered together around the wagon.

"Those I cannot use this time, I'll pay a dollar for coming out here to see us, and Callie has supper for you. Now, here are the ones I've chosen. When I call your name, come stand behind me." He read the names he'd circled on the paper. "That's six, now the rest come collect a dollar and pocket it. Then we'll eat."

They all got paid, then got in line to eat. When all the plates were passed out, Callie told the ones still waiting to let the others eat and then they'd wash the plate and pass out more.

The unfed sat on the ground cross-legged and talked while the others ate.

Callie turned her hands up in defeat and shook her head at Andrew when she finished speaking.

Andrew laughed, amused by her predicament. "You did good. We just don't have that many tin plates. They'll get to eat. You have plenty of food."

"I don't like making them wait."

"It happens." He paused. "You know, Callie, I need to apologize to you."

"What? Why?" She looked confused.

"When we first met, I misjudged you. I was wrong. You're doing a great job for us already. I'm looking forward to seeing you in Los Olivos."

The compliment made her smile—and she really did have a pretty smile. "Thank you."

The next morning, Andrew and Phil woke before dawn and collected their things. It was time to go home and get back to work. Callie had breakfast and coffee waiting for them, and once they'd finished, gave them both a hug.

"Thanks again for letting me come home with you."

They saddled up and said their goodbyes to Jackson, who was busy organizing his new outfit. He tipped his hat, and the half-dozen boys gathered around mimicked him to the last.

Phil laughed. "Those boys are really acting big."

"Yes they are. There aren't many jobs pay money around these days. I never had one. I'd have herded them horses to New York on a paying job when I was that age."

"New York. How far is that, anyway?"

"Maybe two thousand miles or more."

"Whew, a long ways."

"Speaking of a long way, we better trot these horses and push on home. We've got lots to do. I want to go by Mason and get Sophie something nice. She's been holding down the ranch for us and doesn't know if we're dead or alive. She must be sick worrying about it."

"What'll you get her?"

"If I knew that Phil, I'd say I was smart."

"I once wanted to impress a girl in my village. I brought her a pan to cook in. She hit me with it."

"Why?"

"I don't know. Maybe she expected flowers."

Andrew snorted. "I won't take her a pan, then."

They reached Mason mid-morning on the third day. Leaving Phil outside with the horse, he dismounted and visited the dress shop. The owner remembered him and his brother, and Sophie, too. She showed him several dresses she thought would fit her, but none of them looked like Sophie to him. He was just about to give up when the lady brought out a long-tail, bright dress that shined in the light from the window.

"I'll take it."

Wrapped in tissue tied with string, he'd have to carry it, for it would not fit in his saddlebags. Anxious to quickly get home, they short-loped across the country to save time. Using a shortcut through the hills, Andrew charged his horse uphill through some live oak and cedars. As they reached the top, they met three more head-on, each with guns drawn.

Phil cried out a warning.

Andrew wheeled and found himself staring down the barrel of a massive six-gun aimed right at his face. On instinct, he dropped the package with Sophie's dress, drew his Colt, and drove spurs into the big horse's sides. The gelding bellowed and charged into the other rider, knocking the mount off its feet and causing the shot to go wild.

He turned in the saddle, firing his Colt at the other two as fast as he could pull the trigger. Between he and Phil, both went down. Then he noticed a fleeing rider racing away across the flat mountaintop meadow.

McCory.

Son of a bitch!

He spurred the horse again and drove past Phil, who was off his horse and retrieving something from the ground. "I'm going after him."

"Go get him. I'm right behind you!"

All caution thrown to the wind, Andrew crested the ridge and plunged down the other side into another stand of live oak.

A bullet cut through the leaves and chipped a branch near his head. With no idea where the shooter was, he slid the horse to a hard stop and stepped down. He'd be a far less tempting target closer to the ground.

Another shot range out, and the bullet came through the cover above him.

Dammit!

McCory was above and behind him, back up the ridge where Andrew had just come from. In his haste, he'd passed right by him. It was a miracle McCory hadn't simply shot him in the back as he'd gone by.

But things may not have turned out so bad, after all. Shooting down such a steep slope was not as easy as people thought and if McCory really was still up there, that put the man right between him and Phil.

Andrew slid behind a thick oak trunk in the dense vegetation, listening, waiting for another shot. Staying quiet, he dug more ammo out of his pocket and reloaded his Colt, putting fresh caps on the nipples.

Finally, he grew tired of playing the waiting game. "You still up there, McCory? Or did you find your yellow streak again and run off?"

"You're gawdamn right I'm here, Franks." The scratchy

voice echoed off the rock face, then faded into the trees. "And you better you be ready to die 'cause I'm killing your ass today."

Andrew couldn't help but smirk at that. How original. "We took three of your men out already, old man. You really think you've got what it takes to finish me alone?"

"Damn you, boy. You ain't got no backing today. I'm coming to finish you off. Then I'm going to kill that bitch over your ranch that shot at me."

His fingers tightened around the grips of the Colt. At least the old bastard hadn't been back to Turkey Track yet. That meant Sophie was safe, and at that moment, that mattered more than anything in the world he could think of.

Andrew moved to his right, using the trees to shield his movements as he pulled himself back uphill. He had no clear idea just where McCory was yet, though. He needed him to talk more to find him.

"Sounds like you've got it all figured out McCory." He paused. "Except you forgot just one little thing."

"What's that?"

"My partner, Philippé."

"Bullshit, you're bluffing."

Andrew laughed, loud and clear. "Try me."

"Who the hell are you talking about?"

"That would be me, *pendejo*." Phil's voice filtered down from the ledge above. "Now drop the gun or die."

Shots rang out and a scream echoed down the ridge. With an icy ball in his stomach, Andrew sprinted uphill through the tangles of vines and juniper. If that sumbitch had killed Phil....

He tripped over something and went flying. Hitting the ground on his shoulder, he raised the gun and whirled, looking for what he'd fallen over.

It was McCory—bloody, crumpled in a pile in the dirt, a pall of gunsmoke swirling in the branches of the trees above him.

"Phil?"

His bodyguard appeared from above, reloading his pistol as he trudged down the ridge toward him. "Is this the *hombré* you been fighting with?"

"That's him. Guess he won't trouble us anymore."

Phil shook his head and holstered his six-gun. "Leave him for the buzzards, too?"

"He ain't my kin. I'd say so." Andrew put his arm around his friend's shoulder. "McCory was a tough guy like my pa. But he never learned anything. That was his downfall."

"Not like you, *patrón*."

"Not like me."

"Except when it comes to oatmeal." Phil shuddered and made a gagging noise. "Even Sophie says that's a lost cause."

"Ah, damn."

"What is it, *amigo*?"

"Sophie's dress. I dropped it back up on the ridge. I'll have to ride back up and find it."

Phil waved it away. "Naw. That's what I stopped and picked up. It's on my horse."

"Thanks for thinking about me."

"Someone's got to."

Phil went off in search of his horse. Andrew, though, stood rooted to the spot, looking down at McCory's body. Earlier in the day, the feud with the old man had been the furthest thing from his mind—old news compared to the theft of the mustang herd or the upcoming cattle drives to Kansas. And now, here he was, standing over McCory's dead body.

Obviously, the feud hadn't been something the other man could so easily dismiss. He really *had* been like Pa.

Pa.

He looked out through the trees toward the horizon. So much had happened to him and Jackson since they'd buried their parents all those months ago. Strange that he actually felt more loss with McCory's passing than he did with his own Ma and Pa. Did that mean he really *had* grown up?

Or was it something more?

When McCory had him pinned down in the live oak a few minutes before, it hadn't been himself Andrew had been worried about. Or pain. Or even death.

It had been Phil. And Jackson.

And Sophie, most of all.

In other words, it had been the people he cared about most. The people he *loved*, and who loved him, too, without question or condition. Not for what he could do for or give them, but for who he *was*. Andrew Franks.

The Pride of Texas.

Maybe is wasn't that he hadn't felt anything when his parents died. Maybe it was that he felt it more deeply now. Or that he actually understood it. Understood what Sophie meant when she kept saying that. Because now... he had something to lose.

Family.

While he and Jackson had been ranging around the country turning Turkey Track into a real, working ranch trying to prove themselves to everyone who didn't matter, they'd found something they'd never realized they'd missed—a family.

Love.

People like Pa and McCory didn't have what they had. And because they didn't understand that kind of love, they couldn't give it. And so, like dogs marking their territory, they sprayed everyone with their hatred and aggression because they didn't.

This was why the women he encountered made him so uncomfortable, Tasha Miguel included. He didn't need anyone to fill some hole inside him. He got up every morning to do something he loved for the people he loved. Turkey Track and the people who ran it were what mattered most to him. With their help, he'd built a foundation for them and their future. And with McCory now gone, he and Phil had protected them from harm. The score had been settled — fairly, and with honor.

He and Jackson had plans to take two big herds to Kansas next spring. They had some great hands now to help them, and nothing there was nothing between Bexar and Abilene they couldn't mount up and ride over. But it would take a hell of a lot of work in the meantime, and he'd damn sure have little time for anything — or anybody — else.

He wondered again about Tasha. What was she doing right then? Would she still be single when they got back from Kansas? If so, he just might take her to that ball in San Antonio and ask her to marry him... or he might not. It would all depend on if he could figure out whether she wanted *him*, or Turkey Track and what its success represented. But no matter what, the ranch and his family were his life and his priority.

Finally turning away from McCory, he walked down the slope and to his horse and picked the reins up off the rocky ground.

Andrew mounted his horse and headed off west again with Phil at his side. They had miles as yet to ride to get home. Daylight was wasting, and there was a helluva lot of work yet to do before spring.

But before that, he had a pretty new dress to deliver to the woman who had made it all possible.

DUSTY RICHARDS grew up riding horses and watching his western heroes on the big screen. He even wrote book reports for his classmates, making up westerns since English teachers didn't read that kind of book. His mother, though, didn't want him to be a cowboy, so he went to college, then worked for Tyson Foods and auctioned cattle when he wasn't an anchor on television.

His lifelong dream, though, was to write the novels he loved. He sat on the stoop of Zane Grey's cabin and promised he'd one day get published, as well. In 1992, that promise became a reality when his first book, *Noble's Way*, hit the shelves. In the twenty-five years since, he's published over 150 more, winning nearly every major award for western literature along the way.

When he's not writing or traveling the country promoting his work, Dusty also like to fish for trout on the White River.

facebook: westernauthordustyrichards
www.dustyrichards.com

DUSTY RICHARDS

"A Natural Born Storyteller!" —Brett Cogburn

PRESENTS

THE AWARD-WINNING

BRANDIRON

SERIES

Harrowing Tales of Life and Love in the Old West!

A BRIDE FOR GIL

THE MUSTANGER AND THE LADY

THE TEXAS BADGE

THE CHEROKEE STRIP

GOLD IN THE SUN

THE PRIDE OF TEXAS

CPSIA information can be obtained
at www.ICGtesting.com
Printed in the USA
LVOW03s1518090218
565962LV00001B/2/P